Hi, my name's Andy and I live in a
169-storey treehouse with my friends
Terry and Jill. It started as a 13-storey treehouse,
but over the years it has grown so big and we've
met so many different people, animals and things
that it's kind of hard to remember exactly who's
who and what's where—which is why we've
made this book.

Have fun (and pay attention because
there'll be a short quiz at the end)!

ALSO BY ANDY GRIFFITHS
AND ILLUSTRATED BY TERRY DENTON

BARK

# WHO'S WHO and WHAT'S WHERE in the TREEHOUSE

## ANDY GRIFFITHS

### ILLUSTRATED BY
## TERRY DENTON

**PAN**

Pan Macmillan Australia

Pan Macmillan acknowledges the Traditional Custodians of Country throughout Australia and their connections to lands, waters and communities. We pay our respect to Elders past and present and extend that respect to all Aboriginal and Torres Strait Islander peoples today. We honour more than sixty thousand years of storytelling, art and culture.

First published 2023 in Pan by Pan Macmillan Australia Pty Ltd
1 Market Street, Sydney, New South Wales, Australia, 2000

 A catalogue record for this book is available from the National Library of Australia

Typeset in 11.5 / 14 Duper by Seymour Designs
Printed by IVE

 The paper in this book is FSC® certified. FSC® promotes environmentally responsible, socially beneficial and economically viable management of the world's forests.

# CONTENTS

------------------------------------

------------------------------------

# PART ONE
# WHO'S WHO
## ALL the CHARACTERS

It's actually a carrot, Pete.

If you're like most of our readers, you're probably wondering how many characters there are in the Treehouse series and what their likes, dislikes, super powers and threat ratings are. Well then, you are going to *love* this section because that's what it's all about!

Jill! The horses have taken all the pencils.

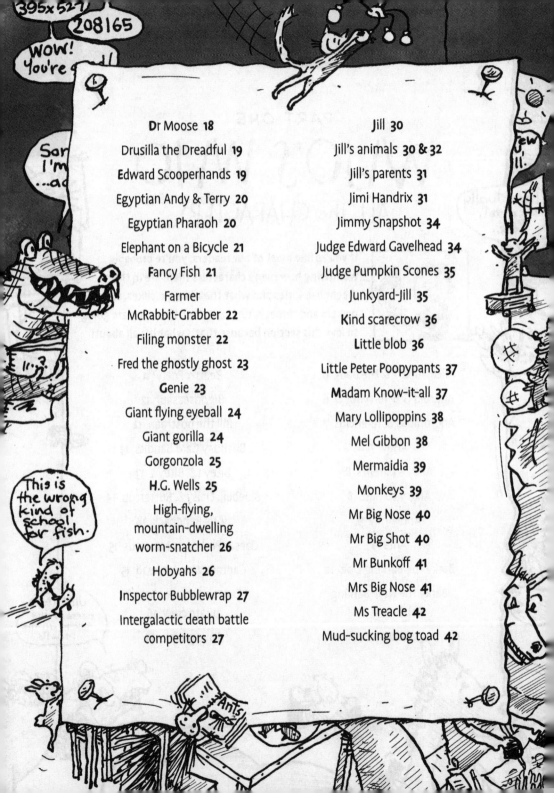

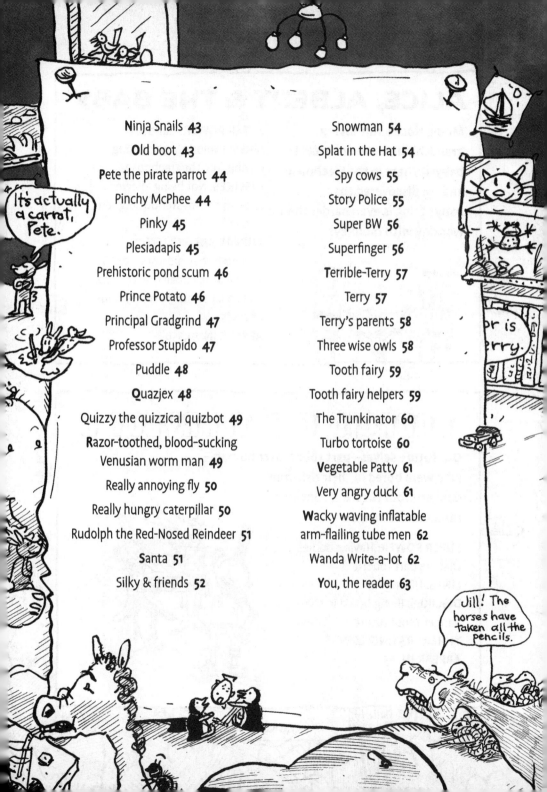

# ALICE, ALBERT & THE BABY

Mr Big Nose's fun-loving grandchildren. We once had to babysit them in the treehouse and we discovered that babysitting is even harder than working with monkeys.

**SUPER POWER:** Curiosity
**LIKES:** Exploring, wandering, having fun, the treehouse
**DISLIKES:** Not being allowed to push the mysterious big red button
**THREAT RATING:** LOW, although they did knock out The Trunkinator, eat all the ice-cream and collapse our 91-storey house of cards
**APPEAR IN:** 91, 156

Albert
Alice
baby

# ANDROID G & TERRYBOT D

Our future selves—part robot, part human—who were bored in their risk-free, danger-proof future . . . until we restored the danger.

**SUPER POWER:** Having bodies that are part robotic
**LIKES:** Having fun
**DISLIKES:** Being bored in the danger-proof future
**THREAT RATING:** LOW
**APPEAR IN:** 65

Hello!

WHO'S WHO

# ANDRONICUS & TERENCIUS

Our brave Roman ancestors who helped us win a chariot race against Drusilla the Dreadful. All hail us!

**SUPER POWER:** Chariot racing
**LIKES:** Winning chariot races
**DISLIKES:** Being put to death for losing chariot races
**THREAT RATING:** LOW
**APPEAR IN:** 65

---

ANDY

book

That's me! I live in a 169-storey treehouse, write books and have adventures with my friends Terry and Jill.

**SUPER POWER:** Storytelling
**LIKES:** Writing books, reading books, having adventures with my friends Terry and Jill
**DISLIKES:** Stories with morals or lessons; being shouted at by our publisher, Mr Big Nose
**THREAT RATING:** LOW, unless you attempt to steal my chips
**APPEARS IN:** All books (obviously), especially MY AUTOBIOGRAPHY OF MY LIFE BY ME (AND NOT TERRY) (78)

Giraffe noise.

# ANDY'S PARENTS

Sure, they look harmless enough, but my parents were super strict. For example, they made me wear clothes, eat with a knife and fork and go to school FIVE days a week! (Which is why I had no choice but to run away from home.)

parents

rules

**SUPER POWER:** Making up rules
**LIKES:** Rules, spoiling other people's fun
**DISLIKES:** Fun
**THREAT RATING:** HIGH. Too many rules!
**APPEAR IN:** 26

# ANGRY TOMATO

Guardian of the
Vegetable Kingdom and
charged with the task
of preventing non-vegetables
from entering.

VEGETABLES ONLY PAST THIS POINT

**SUPER POWER:** Knowledge of the United States Supreme Court ruling on whether tomatoes are considered a vegetable or fruit
**LIKES:** Vegetables, rules, laws relating to vegetables
**DISLIKES:** Non-vegetables and people who call tomatoes a fruit
**THREAT RATING:** MEDIUM
**APPEARS IN:** 52

Hello!

WHO'S WHO

# ANTI-ANDY

Anti-Andy is my trouble-making doppelganger. He escaped from our doppelganger mirror with his friends Junkyard-Jill and Terrible-Terry.

**SUPER POWER:** Being anti everything
**LIKES:** Fellow members of the mirror gang, Terrible-Terry and Junkyard-Jill, and calling people chumps
**DISLIKES:** Reading books, writing books, school, monkeys, Mr Big Nose
**THREAT RATING:** MEDIUM
**APPEARS IN:** 169

**Residents of the 65-chamber ant farm in the treehouse.**

**SUPER POWER:** Ability to work together to form themselves into any shape imaginable
**LIKES:** A peaceful life
**DISLIKES:** Anteaters, and having their ant farm destroyed by our irresponsible use of bowling balls, rocking horses and chainsaws
**THREAT RATING:** LOW, unless angered (*see* Dislikes)
**APPEAR IN:** 65

Giraffe noise.

# BARKY The Barking Dog

Star of Terry's favourite TV show—*The Barky the Barking Dog Show*. (Possibly the most boring show ever made.)

**SUPER POWER:** Barking

**LIKES:** Barking

**DISLIKES:** Not barking (and giant gorillas)

**THREAT RATING:** LOW, though you are in danger of dying of boredom watching this incredibly boring show (unless you're Terry)

**APPEARS IN:** 13

# BARKY THE NON-BARKING ROBO-DOG

non-bark →

The non-barking robo-dog star of the futuristic *The Barky the Non-Barking Robo-Dog Show*. (Believe it or not, it's even more boring than *The Barky the Barking Dog Show!*)

**SUPER POWER:** Non-barking

**LIKES:** Not barking

**DISLIKES:** Barking

**THREAT RATING:** LOW, though you are in even more danger of dying of boredom watching this show than the original

**APPEARS IN:** 65

Hello!

# BEARS

Honey-loving, fridge- and bun-throwing bears that overran the treehouse when Terry accidentally flooded it with honey.

**SUPER POWER:** Strength, ability to eat large amounts of honey

**LIKES:** Eating honey, throwing fridges and buns, having bedtime stories read to them

**DISLIKES:** Missing out on their bedtime story

**THREAT RATING:** MEDIUM

**APPEAR IN:** 104

# BEATRIX POTTY

Author and illustrator of *The Tale of Little Peter Poopypants*, the story of a mischievous little rabbit that likes to eat the vegetables in Farmer McRabbit-Grabber's garden. (*See also* Little Peter Poopypants)

**SUPER POWER:** Storytelling and illustrating

**LIKES:** Animals (especially rabbits)

**DISLIKES:** Rabbit-hating farmers

**THREAT RATING:** LOW

**APPEARS IN:** 117

flower pot

The Tale of Little Peter Poopypants

story and pictures by Beatrix Potty

Giraffe noise.

# BIGNOSEASAUR

A ferocious dinosaur with a really big nose that bears a striking resemblance—both in appearance and temperament—to our publisher, Mr Big Nose.

ferocious roar

**SUPER POWER:** Being a ferocious dinosaur
**LIKES:** Roaring, charging, eating
**DISLIKES:** Becoming extinct

**THREAT RATING:** EXTREME, in fact, when its nose exploded the blast was responsible for wiping out all the other dinosaurs on Earth
**APPEARS IN:** 65

## Bill the POSTMAN

An extremely dedicated and hardworking postman who delivers all our mail. Bill can deliver mail anywhere, even into outer space!

**SUPER POWER:** Delivering mail
**LIKES:** Delivering mail and being helpful
**DISLIKES:** Dogs, birds and those enemies of postal workers everywhere—the Birthday Card Bandits
**THREAT RATING:** LOW
**APPEARS IN:** 13, 26, 39, 52, 65, 91, 104, 130, 143, 156, Treehouse Tales

Hello!

# BIRTHDAY CARD BANDITS

A gang of postal-worker-impersonating thieves feared by postal workers, grandparents and children throughout the land.

**SUPER POWER:** Sneakiness
**LIKES:** Intercepting birthday cards, crashing birthday parties and stealing balloons, presents and wishes
**DISLIKES:** Maze of Doom
**THREAT RATING:** EXTREME, if you are a postal worker or a child celebrating your birthday
**APPEAR IN:** 39

# Bitey 1 & Bitey 2

Junkyard-Jill's junkyard guard dogs.

**SUPER POWER:** Biting
**LIKES:** Biting, growling, snarling
**DISLIKES:** Junkyard thieves
**THREAT RATING:** HIGH, especially if you like stealing junk
**APPEAR IN:** 169

Giraffe noise.

# Bluebell, Daisy & Buttercup

Cud-chewing stars of *Cowhouse: The Mooo-vie*, which is the movie that the spy cows made after they stole all our ideas!

**SUPER POWER:** Plagiarism
**LIKES:** The bright lights of showbiz
**DISLIKES:** Coming up with their own ideas
**THREAT RATING:** HIGH, if you have good ideas they might like to steal
**APPEAR IN:** 78

# BORIS BENDBACK

Author and illustrator of *Where the Filed Things Are*, the story of the filing monster who lives on Filing Island and files everything—animals, plants, people, scenery. (*See also* Filing monster)

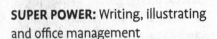

**SUPER POWER:** Writing, illustrating and office management
**LIKES:** Being punched by The Trunkinator, smashing watermelons
**DISLIKES:** The Story Police
**THREAT RATING:** LOW
**APPEARS IN:** 117

Hello!

# CAESAR PROBOSCIS MAXIMUS

Ancient Roman emperor with a big nose, who, like the Bignoseasaur, bears a strong resemblance to Mr Big Nose.

**SUPER POWER:** His thumbs
**LIKES:** Togas, having power over others, speaking Latin
**DISLIKES:** People who lose chariot races; Gauls, Britons, Visigoths and Vandals
**THREAT RATING:** EXTREME, if he gives you the thumbs up, you live; if he gives you the thumbs down, you die
**APPEARS IN:** 65

Note the BIG nose. ←

# CAPTAIN WOODENHEAD

A ruthless pirate, who, after his original head was bitten off by the giant fish Gorgonzola, carved himself a new head out of wood. Attempted to take over the treehouse with his accident-prone pirate crew. (See pages 16–17 for details.)

**SUPER POWER:** Pirating, head carving
**LIKES:** Treasure
**DISLIKES:** Having his head bitten off, Gorgonzola
**THREAT RATING:** EXTREME
**APPEARS IN:** 26

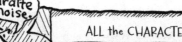

Giraffe noise.

# CAPTAIN WOODENHEAD'S PIRATE CREW

Captain Woodenhead is not only the most fearsome pirate to sail the seven seas, he has (well, he had) the most fearsome (and unlucky) pirate crew sailing with him.

Eeeee-yaahhhhhhhhhh

NAME: Poopdeck Puffypants
CAUSE OF DEATH: Fell off a vine

NAME: Cannonball Connor
CAUSE OF DEATH: Fell through the ice

THUMP!

NAME: Doofus Dave
CAUSE OF DEATH: Bucked off a mechanical bull

Hello!

NAME: Bill Bones
CAUSE OF DEATH: Electric guitar electrocution

NAME: Shortsighted Sam
CAUSE OF DEATH: Missed the pool

NAME: Greedy George
CAUSE OF DEATH: Brain freeze

NAME: Flying Frank
CAUSE OF DEATH: Catapult mishap

SLURP!

NAME: Toothless Ted
CAUSE OF DEATH: Automatic Tattoo Machine malfunction

NAME: Dirty Danny
CAUSE OF DEATH: Baked in mud

# CAVE PEOPLE

Stone Age ancestors of humans who lived in caves and didn't have much to do because none of the cool stuff that we have these days had been invented yet.

**SUPER POWER:** Grunting, asking simple questions
**LIKES:** Caves, clothes made of animal skins
**DISLIKES:** Waiting for computer games and YouTube to be invented
**THREAT RATING:** LOW, but watch out for their clubs
**APPEAR IN:** 65

# DR MOOSE

A doctor and an author–illustrator. His most famous book is *The Splat in the Hat*, a rhyming story about a mess-making splat.
(*See also* Splat in the Hat)

**SUPER POWER:** The power to heal and to rhyme
**LIKES:** Healing, rhyming and running free
**DISLIKES:** Words that don't rhyme
**THREAT RATING:** LOW
**APPEARS IN:** 117, 130

Hello!

# Drusilla The DREADFUL

**The most feared and ruthless charioteer in Ancient Rome, who we had to race in our wheelie bin time machine.**

**SUPER POWER:** Chariot racing
**LIKES:** Winning chariot races by destroying her competitors' chariots with her spiked wheels
**DISLIKES:** Losing chariot races
**THREAT RATING:** EXTREME
**APPEARS IN:** 65

Drusilla    us

spiked wheel

# EDWARD SCOOPERHANDS

hot ice-cream

**SUPER POWER:** Being able to dispense hot or cold ice-cream at high speed
**LIKES:** Serving ice-cream
**DISLIKES:** People who take too long to choose a flavour
**THREAT RATING:** LOW, but beware of brain-freeze from eating his super-cold ice-cream or tongue-burn from eating his super-hot ice-cream
**APPEARS IN:** 26, 52, 91, 130, 143, 156

**The friendly ice-cream serving robot who runs the 78-flavour ice-cream parlour in our treehouse. Married to Mary Lollipoppins.**

Giraffe noise.

# EGYPTIAN ANDY & TERRY

Ancient Egyptian Barky →

Our Ancient Egyptian ancestors who saved us from the Egyptian Pharaoh's guards.

**SUPER POWER:** Super-fast map-making
**LIKES:** Drawing hieroglyphs
**DISLIKES:** The pharaoh's guards
**THREAT RATING:** LOW
**APPEAR IN:** 65

# EGYPTIAN PHARAOH

Ruler of Ancient Egypt who got angry when we accidentally landed our wheelie bin time machine on top of him.

**SUPER POWER:** Pyramid building
**LIKES:** Building pyramids
**DISLIKES:** Visitors from the future, especially building inspectors who question his pyramid-building methods
**THREAT RATING:** EXTREME, he can have you seized by guards and put to death
**APPEARS IN:** 65

Hello!

# Elephant on a Bicycle

The accident-prone star of one of our favourite TV shows, *Elephant on a Bicycle*.

Crumbs!

**SUPER POWER:** Ability to ride a bicycle (it's not easy for an elephant)
**LIKES:** Bicycle riding
**DISLIKES:** Falling off a bicycle
**THREAT RATING:** HIGH, especially if you are in its path, in which case you should get out of the way, fast!
**APPEARS IN:** 130

# FANCY FISH

Extremely fancy proprietor of the Two-Million-Dollar Shop—nothing under two million dollars!

**SUPER POWER:** Ability to raise prices without warning
**LIKES:** High prices and making high prices even higher
**DISLIKES:** Low prices
**THREAT RATING:** LOW, unlike his prices!
**APPEARS IN:** 104, 143

Giraffe noise.

# FARMER McRABBIT-GRABBER

A rabbit-hating farmer in Beatrix Potty's book *The Tale of Little Peter Poopypants*.

**SUPER POWER:** Rabbit grabbing
**LIKES:** Grabbing rabbits and using them to make rabbit pie
**DISLIKES:** Rabbits, pies made of rabbit poop
**THREAT RATING:** EXTREME, if you are a rabbit, or if he thinks you are a rabbit
**APPEARS IN:** 117

# FILING MONSTER

Main character in Boris Bendback's book *Where the Filed Things Are*. The filing monster loves the alphabet and will file anything— animal, mineral or vegetable!

**SUPER POWER:** Alphabetising and filing
**LIKES:** Filed things
**DISLIKES:** Unfiled things
**THREAT RATING:** HIGH
**APPEARS IN:** 117

Hello!

WHO'S WHO

# Fred the Ghostly Ghost

**Whooo, whooo!**

The ghost of a man named Fred, who, after dying and becoming a ghost, dies again . . . and again . . . and again . . . and again, thus becoming the ghost of a ghost of a ghost of a ghost.

**SUPER POWER:** Dying
**LIKES:** Haunting
**DISLIKES:** Bedheads, wind turbines, rivers, dragons
**THREAT RATING:** LOW, unless you're scared of ghosts
**APPEARS IN:** 143

# GENIE

magic lamp

Lives in a magic lamp and grants three wishes to whoever releases it by rubbing the lamp.

**SUPER POWER:** Making wishes come true
**LIKES:** Saying 'Your wish is my command.'
**DISLIKES:** Being imprisoned in a magic lamp
**THREAT RATING:** LOW
**APPEARS IN:** 91

Giraffe noise.

# GIANT FLYING EYEBALL

Giant eyeball from the planet Eyeballia that abducted Terry, Jill and me with the intention of making us take part in an intergalactic death battle. (*See also* Intergalactic death battle competitors)

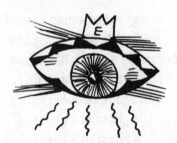

**SUPER POWER:** Abducting aliens from all over the universe and forcing them to fight one another
**LIKES:** Watching aliens fight
**DISLIKES:** Soap bubbles
**THREAT RATING:** EXTREME
**APPEARS IN:** 130

# GIANT GORILLA

A giant-banana-loving inhabitant of a remote island that nearly shakes our tree to pieces after mistaking it for a giant-banana tree.

**SUPER POWER:** Strong sense of smell and super strength
**LIKES:** Bananas, the bigger the better
**DISLIKES:** Barking dogs and flying cats
**THREAT RATING:** EXTREME, especially if it is shaking your tree
**APPEARS IN:** 13

Hello!

WHO'S WHO

# GORGONZOLA

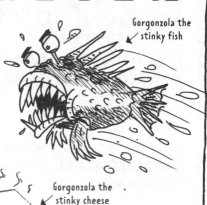

Gorgonzola the stinky fish

The greediest and most disgusting fish in the ocean, it's named after the stinky cheese it smells like.

**SUPER POWER:** Its disgusting smell and huge mouth
**LIKES:** Swimming around eating everything in its path
**DISLIKES:** Captain Woodenhead
**THREAT RATING:** EXTREME
**APPEARS IN:** 26

Gorgonzola the stinky cheese

# H.G. WELLS

Famous time-travelling author from the past. Terry and I gave him the idea to write his most famous book, *The Time Machine*, when we met him in the future.

**SUPER POWER:** Writing science fiction, time-travelling
**LIKES:** Meeting fellow writers who are also time-travellers
**DISLIKES:** Giant crabs
**THREAT RATING:** LOW
**APPEARS IN:** 65

Giraffe noise.

# HigH-flying, mountain-dwelling worm-Snatcher

**Large bird that likes to fly high, dwell near the top of mountains and snatch worms.**

**SUPER POWER:** Flying high
**LIKES:** Worms
**DISLIKES:** Anything or anyone threatening its chicks
**THREAT RATING:** HIGH, if you are a worm or threatening its chicks
**APPEARS IN:** 104

# Hobyahs

HOBYAH!

HOBYAH!

HO BYAH!

sack →

← stick

**Horrible little creatures that like to sneak about at night, grab people, put them in sacks and poke them with sticks while chanting 'Hobyah, Hobyah, Hobyah'.**

**SUPER POWER:** Stealth
**LIKES:** Sneaking, grabbing, bagging, poking, chanting
**DISLIKES:** Being kicked, ghosts
**THREAT RATING:** EXTREME, at night; LOW, during the day
**APPEAR IN:** 143

Hello!

# INSPECTOR BUBBLEWRAP

Safety inspector who came to the treehouse to check if we had a valid building permit. Later became a stuntman and changed his name to Super BW.

safety helmet →

**SUPER POWER:** Comprehensive knowledge of building regulations and safety codes
**LIKES:** Bubblewrap, fences, wheelchair ramps, guardrails, handrails, warning signs, safety blankets, fire extinguishers, exit plans
**DISLIKES:** Senseless risk-taking
**THREAT RATING:** HIGH, if your treehouse doesn't have a building permit
**APPEARS IN:** 65

rules & regulations →

## INTERGALACTIC DEATH BATTLE COMPETITORS

After being abducted by a giant flying eyeball, we were taken to Eyeballia to participate in an intergalactic death battle against twelve other alien species. Turn the page for a full list of the competitors ... if you dare!

Giraffe noise.

# INTERGALACTIC DEATH BATTLE COMPETITORS

**SPACE COW**
HOME PLANET: The Moo-n
SUPER POWER: Biting

**SCREAMING MEEMEE**
HOME PLANET: Vociferacio
SUPER POWER: Ear-piercing scream

**TANGLER**
HOME PLANET: Tutania
SUPER POWER: Tangling

**GUT GOBBLER**
HOME PLANET: Vomitene
SUPER POWER: Gobbling guts

**FLAME LIZARD**
HOME PLANET: Congflagoria
SUPER POWER: Fire breath

**MANGLER**
HOME PLANET: Mutilatio
SUPER POWER: Mangling

Hello!

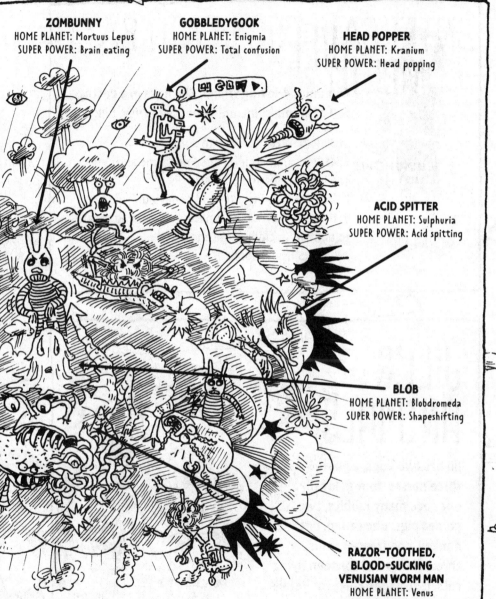

**ZOMBUNNY**
HOME PLANET: Mortuus Lepus
SUPER POWER: Brain eating

**GOBBLEDYGOOK**
HOME PLANET: Enigmia
SUPER POWER: Total confusion

**HEAD POPPER**
HOME PLANET: Kranium
SUPER POWER: Head popping

**ACID SPITTER**
HOME PLANET: Sulphuria
SUPER POWER: Acid spitting

**BLOB**
HOME PLANET: Blobdromeda
SUPER POWER: Shapeshifting

**RAZOR-TOOTHED,
BLOOD-SUCKING
VENUSIAN WORM MAN**
HOME PLANET: Venus
SUPER POWER: Blood sucking

ALL the CHARACTERS

# JiLL

↑
Silky

Our animal-loving friend. She lives in a cottage full of animals, including her favourite, Silky.

**SUPER POWER:** Can talk to animals
**LIKES:** All animals (except spiders), me and Terry, solving puzzles and problems
**DISLIKES:** Mean and unkind behaviour
**THREAT RATING:** LOW, unless you're being mean to animals (including me and Terry)
**APPEARS IN:** All books

# JiLL'S ANIMALS

Jill has two dogs, a goat, three horses, four goldfish, one cow, many rabbits, two guinea pigs, one camel, one donkey, one frogpotamus, three snakes and thirteen flying cats. (See pages 32–33 for details. *See also* Silky & friends.)

Hello!

# JILL'S PARENTS

Socialites mainly interested in hosting parties on their luxury superyacht who didn't even notice when Jill fell overboard. They were last seen inside the belly of Gorgonzola.

parents

fancy friends

superyacht

**SUPER POWER:** Partying
**LIKES:** Parties, champagne, superyachts, fancy friends
**DISLIKES:** Animals
**THREAT RATING:** LOW
**APPEAR IN:** 26

# JIMI HANDRIX

A singer and guitarist, famous for his epic guitar playing. He is Superfinger's favourite guitarist.

**SUPER POWER:** Guitar playing
**LIKES:** Singing and playing guitar
**DISLIKES:** Not having an extra finger to make his guitar solos even more epic
**THREAT RATING:** LOW, unless you don't like epic guitar solos
**APPEARS IN:** 13, 39

Giraffe noise.

# JILL'S ANIMALS

**MOE**
TYPE: Horse
SUPER POWER: Cheating at cards

**SILKY**
TYPE: Cat
SUPER POWER: Flying

**LARRY**
TYPE: Horse
SUPER POWER: Galloping

**CURLY**
TYPE: Horse
SUPER POWER: Neighing

**MR HEE-HAW**
TYPE: Donkey
SUPER POWER: Hee-hawing

**MANNY**
TYPE: Goat
SUPER POWER: Cooking

Hello!

**BILL & PHIL**
TYPE: Guinea pigs
SUPER POWER: Squeaking

**PAT**
TYPE: Cow
SUPER POWER: Mooing

**THE FISH PISTOLS**
TYPE: Goldfish
SUPER POWER: Punk rock

**FROGPOTAMUS**
TYPE: Half frog, half hippo
SUPER POWER: Jumping

**LAIKA**
TYPE: Dog
SUPER POWER: Tail wagging

**LOOMPY**
TYPE: Dog
SUPER POWER: Licking

**PINK**
TYPE: Camel
SUPER POWER: Spitting

**SLIDEY, SLITHERY & ROGER**
TYPE: Snakes
SUPER POWER: Hissing

# Jimmy Snapshot

Photographer who works for *Go Away!* travel magazine and comes to the treehouse with journalist Wanda Write-a-lot to do a story on our camping holiday.

camera

**SUPER POWER:** Taking photos
**LIKES:** Taking photos
**DISLIKES:** People who shut their eyes when he's taking their photo
**THREAT RATING:** LOW
**APPEARS IN:** 143, 169

# JUDGE EDWARD GAVELHEAD

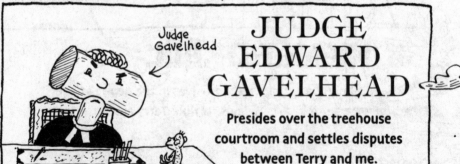

Judge Gavelhead

Presides over the treehouse courtroom and settles disputes between Terry and me.

**SUPER POWER:** Using his head as a gavel
**LIKES:** Banging his head on the bench and shouting 'Order in the court!'
**DISLIKES:** Getting a headache from continually banging his head on the bench and shouting 'Order in the court!'
**THREAT RATING:** LOW, as long as you are law-abiding
**APPEARS IN:** 78

Hello!

# JUDGE PUMPKIN SCONES

**Judges cases brought to the bench by the Story Police.**

**SUPER POWER:** Superior literary discrimination
**LIKES:** Stories with conventional plot structure, well-rounded characters and no unnecessary repetition (i.e. NO UNNECESSARY REPETITION)
**DISLIKES:** Our books
**THREAT RATING:** LOW, unless you're us in which case there is a high chance you will be sent to storytelling jail for a billion years
**APPEARS IN:** 117

# JUNKYARD-JILL

**Jill's junk-loving doppelganger who lives in the doppelganger mirror with her mirror gang pals Terrible-Terry and Anti-Andy.**

**SUPER POWER:** Super strength
**LIKES:** Junk and her dogs Bitey 1 & Bitey 2
**DISLIKES:** People who try to steal her junk
**THREAT RATING:** LOW, unless you're trying to steal her junk
**APPEARS IN:** 169

Giraffe noise.

# KIND SCARECROW

A non-scary scarecrow that is supposed to guard our toffee-apple orchard but doesn't do a very good job because it's too kind to say no to anybody who wants to pick a toffee apple.

**SUPER POWER:** Kindness to children
**LIKES:** Children, toffee apples, telling ghost stories
**DISLIKES:** Unkindness to children
**THREAT RATING:** LOW
**APPEARS IN:** 143

## Little BLOB

A shapeshifting, mud-dwelling, mud-eating, mudpie-making alien from the planet Blobdromeda.

**SUPER POWER:** Ability to stretch and mould itself into any form
**LIKES:** Mud and singing about mud
**DISLIKES:** Mud-sucking bog toads, drying out in the sun, intergalactic death battles
**THREAT RATING:** LOW
**APPEARS IN:** 130

Hello!

# Little Peter
# POOPYPANTS

The main character in Beatrix Potty's book *The Tale of Little Peter Poopypants*. Obsessed with eating Farmer McRabbit-Grabber's vegetables.

**SUPER POWER:** Pooping
**LIKES:** Vegetables
**DISLIKES:** Farmer McRabbit-Grabber
**THREAT RATING:** LOW, unless you're one of Farmer McRabbit-Grabber's vegetables
**APPEARS IN:** 117

# *Madam Know-it-all*

An evil fortune teller who escaped from a high-security travelling carnival and set up a fortune-telling tent in our treehouse.

**SUPER POWERS:** Fortune telling and brain draining
**LIKES:** Draining people's brains to gain more knowledge
**DISLIKES:** Not knowing every possible thing that there is to know
**THREAT RATING:** EXTREME, do not ask her a question!
**APPEARS IN:** 78, 91

crystal ball

Giraffe noise.

# MARY LOLLIPOPPINS

A lovely lollipop lady who runs the treehouse lollipop shop, which has lollipops from the past, present and future. Married to Edward Scooperhands.

**SUPER POWER:** Loves lollipops and knows how to use them
**LIKES:** All types of lollipops
**DISLIKES:** Dentists
**THREAT RATING:** LOW, unless you're a tooth
**APPEARS IN:** 65, 130, 143

# MEL GIBBON

A really annoying monkey that was cast in the role of Andy in *Treehouse: The Movie* after the film's director Mr Big Shot sacked me.

**SUPER POWER:** Imitating—and annoying—me
**LIKES:** Stealing movie roles and best friends
**DISLIKES:** Being called a monkey (he's actually a gibbon, apparently)
**THREAT RATING:** HIGH, if you have a best friend or a part in a movie
**APPEARS IN:** 78

Hello!

WHO'S WHO

Hello!

# MERMAIDIA

mermaid disguise

A horrible, slimy sea monster who, after pretending to be a mermaid and tricking Terry into marrying her, tried to eat both of us.

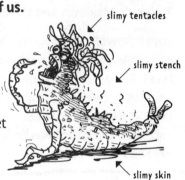

slimy tentacles

slimy stench

slimy skin

**SUPER POWER:** Being able to disguise herself as a mermaid
**LIKES:** Eating humans
**DISLIKES:** Being shrunk with a shrinking ray and flushed down the toilet
**THREAT RATING:** EXTREME
**APPEARS IN:** 13, Treehouse Tales

# MONKEYS

Monkeys are the worst! They come into your treehouse or school and make a huge mess and wreck everything. We hate them.

**SUPER POWER:** Creating mayhem
**LIKES:** Making mess, wrecking everything, bananas
**DISLIKES:** Being called gibbons
**THREAT RATING:** HIGH, if you live in a treehouse or are at school
**APPEAR IN:** 13, 169

Giraffe noise.

# MR BIG NOSE

A very busy business man. He runs Big Nose Books, which publishes our books. (Bears a strong resemblance to the Bignoseasaur, Caesar Proboscis Maximus and the Egyptian Pharaoh.)

**SUPER POWER:** Shouting, and he also has a good nose for knowing what books will sell
**LIKES:** Being busy and shouting at Terry and me
**DISLIKES:** People wasting his very important time (i.e. mainly Terry and me)
**THREAT RATING:** HIGH, because the angrier he gets, the bigger his nose gets, and it has been known to grow so large that it explodes
**APPEARS IN:** All books

# Mr BIG Shot

A big shot Hollywood director who came to the treehouse to direct *Treehouse: The Movie* but, sadly, sacked me, made Terry the star and wouldn't listen when I tried to warn him about the spy cows that were trying to steal all our ideas.

**SUPER POWER:** Directing
**LIKES:** Shouting 'Action!'
**DISLIKES:** Movies with too much talking, not enough action; narrators
**THREAT RATING:** LOW
**APPEARS IN:** 78

Hello!

40

Hello!

# MR BUNKOFF

Truancy officer who captured
Terry, Jill and me and forced
us to attend school.

**SUPER POWER:** Detecting children who
are not enrolled in school
**LIKES:** Children to be at school
**DISLIKES:** Children who are not at school
**THREAT RATING:** HIGH, if you are a child
who is not at school
**APPEARS IN:** 169

# MRS BIG NOSE

**Wife of Mr Big Nose, our publisher, and
grandmother of Alice, Albert and the baby.**

**SUPER POWER:** Being able to put
up with Mr Big Nose
**LIKES:** The opera, her grandchildren,
Mr Big Nose
**DISLIKES:** Anything bad happening
to her grandchildren
**THREAT RATING:** LOW
**APPEARS IN:** 91, 156

Giraffe
noise.

ALL the CHARACTERS

# Ms Treacle

Our classroom teacher when we were captured by Mr Bunkoff and made to attend school.

**SUPER POWER:** Patience
**LIKES:** School
**DISLIKES:** Monkey mayhem, students' underpants inflating during class time
**THREAT RATING:** LOW
**APPEARS IN:** 169

# Mud-Sucking BOG TOAD

Lives on the planet Blobdromeda and loves to eat mud, especially if the mud is made into a mud pie.

**SUPER POWER:** Ability to suck up huge amounts of mud
**LIKES:** Mud, especially if made into a pie
**DISLIKES:** Not getting a mud pie when it has been promised one
**THREAT RATING:** EXTREME, if you live in mud
**APPEARS IN:** 130

Hello!

Hello!

# NINJA SNAILS

**An elite fighting force of snails trained by Terry in his Ninja Snail Training Academy.**

**SUPER POWER:** Moving so slowly that an opponent can barely detect any movement at all
**LIKES:** Throwing Ninja death-stars, lighting decoy fires, solving Ninja crossword puzzles, relaxing in the spa after training sessions
**DISLIKES:** Feet, birds, French chefs
**THREAT RATING:** HIGH
**APPEAR IN:** 52

## OLD BOOT

CLOMP!

**Accidentally hooked while fishing on our camping holiday. It helped us defeat the hobyahs and now spends its days hanging out with all its old-boot pals on our old boot camp level.**

**SUPER POWER:** Kicking hobyahs
**LIKES:** Relaxing by the fire, spinning yarns with other old boots
**DISLIKES:** Hobyahs
**THREAT RATING:** LOW, unless you're a hobyah
**APPEARS IN:** 143, 156

Giraffe noise.

# pete the pirate parrot

Found filed under P in a filing cabinet on Filing Island. On his release, he stole our dot yacht and sailed away.

eye patch

**SUPER POWER:** Parrot-powered piracy
**LIKES:** Stealing
**DISLIKES:** Being put in a filing cabinet
**THREAT RATING:** LOW, unless you are the owner of a dot yacht
**APPEARS IN:** 117

# PINCHY Mc PHEE

Extremely friendly shopkeeper who runs the Two-Dollar Shop— nothing over two dollars!

**SUPER POWER:** Customer service
**LIKES:** Singing about what he has to sell in his shop
**DISLIKES:** High prices
**THREAT RATING:** LOW, LOW, LOW, just like his prices!
**APPEARS IN:** 104, 143

Hello!

Hello!

# PiNKY

Faithful sidekick of superhero Superfinger.

**SUPER POWER:** Helping Superfinger provide finger-based solutions to finger-based problems
**LIKES:** Solving problems, playing tambourine
**DISLIKES:** Paper-cuts
**THREAT RATING:** LOW
**APPEARS IN:** 13

# PLESIADAPIS

The world's first mammals. Terry and I met two that looked a bit like us when we travelled back in time in our wheelie bin time machine.

**SUPER POWER:** Surviving catastrophic explosions (e.g. the day the Bignoseasaur's nose exploded)
**LIKES:** Staying safe in their burrows
**DISLIKES:** Bignoseasaurs
**THREAT RATING:** LOW
**APPEAR IN:** 65

looks a bit like me, Andy

looks a bit like Terry

Giraffe noise.

# PREHISTORIC POND SCUM

Simple forms of life from which all life forms subsequently evolved. Lived in prehistoric ponds billions of years ago.

**SUPER POWER:** Being the first organisms on Earth
**LIKES:** Moisture, shade
**DISLIKES:** Excessive sunlight, clumsy fools (e.g. Terry)
**THREAT RATING:** LOW
**APPEAR IN:** 65

## Prince POTATO

Ruler of the Vegetable Kingdom. He captured Mr Big Nose, Terry, Jill and me and tried to make us into human soup.

**SUPER POWER:** Commands an army of ferocious fighting vegetables
**LIKES:** Carrot princesses, revenge
**DISLIKES:** Humans, especially Terry, Jill, Mr Big Nose, Vegetable Patty and me
**THREAT RATING:** EXTREME
**APPEARS IN:** 52

Hello!

Hello!

# PRINCIPAL GRADGRIND

Rule-obsessed principal who built a school
with nothing but the sweat of his brow
and a book called *How to Build a School
With Nothing But the Sweat of Your Brow
and This Book.*

**SUPER POWER:** Enforcing school rules
**LIKES:** Rules, books (non-fiction only)
**DISLIKES:** Having his school destroyed by monkeys
**THREAT RATING:** LOW, unless you've broken the
rules or are a monkey that has destroyed his school
**APPEARS IN:** 169

# PROFESSOR STUPIDO

The world's greatest un-inventor.
With a simple rhyme and a zap from his
finger, he can un-invent anything on the spot.

wild eyes    crazy hair

**SUPER POWER:** Un-inventing things
**LIKES:** Dancing, rhyming, un-inventing things that annoy him
**DISLIKES:** Once-upon-a-time machines;
flying beetroots; The Trunkinator; people;
the Earth; the universe; pretty much everything, really
**THREAT RATING:** EXTREME
**APPEARS IN:** 39, Treehouse Tales

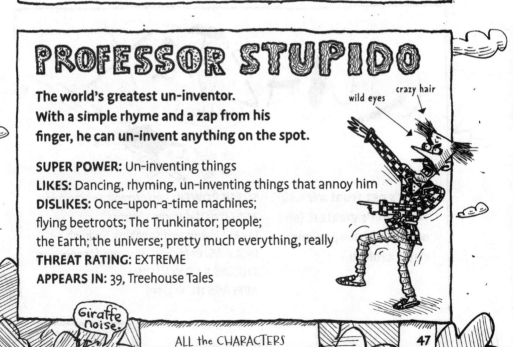

Giraffe
noise.

# PUDDLE

A large, hostile body of water that threatened to drown me and empuddle the treehouse. Fortunately, I'm an experienced puddle fighter and was able to suck it all up before it could do any real harm.

**SUPER POWER:** Ability to empuddle the world
**LIKES:** Drowning its enemies
**DISLIKES:** Sunshine, puddle fighters and straws
**THREAT RATING:** EXTREME, to all non-aquatic life forms
**APPEARS IN:** 78

# QUAZJEX

¡Hola!

Terry's pet stunt axolotl. The world's greatest (and only) Spanish-speaking stunt axolotl!

**SUPER POWER:** Performing spectacular and often dangerous stunts
**LIKES:** Flying and speaking Spanish
**DISLIKES:** Being out of water for too long
**THREAT RATING:** LOW
**APPEARS IN:** 143, 156

Hello!

Hello!

# QUIZZY
## THE QUIZZICAL QUIZBOT

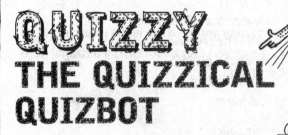

Host of the treehouse's TV quiz show level, Quizzy just loves asking questions (well, that's what he's programmed to do).

**SUPER POWER:** Asking questions
**LIKES:** The sound of buzzers
**DISLIKES:** Killer robots
**THREAT RATING:** LOW
**APPEARS IN:** 156

## Razor-Toothed, Blood-Sucking Venusian Worm Man

Suck! Suck! Suck! Suck!

Terrifying alien from the planet Venus that has razor-sharp teeth and likes to suck blood. One of the intergalactic death battle competitors we faced when kidnapped by the giant flying eyeball from Eyeballia.

**SUPER POWER:** Killing
**LIKES:** Sucking blood
**DISLIKES:** Having hot ice-cream thrown at it
**THREAT RATING:** EXTREME
**APPEARS IN:** 39, 130

Giraffe noise.

# REALLY ANNOYING FLY

A really annoying fly that really annoyed me while I was trying to narrate *The 130-Storey Treehouse*. Later adopted as a national hero by the citizens of Blobdromeda.

**SUPER POWER:** Buzzing loudly
**LIKES:** Being worshipped by Blobs
**DISLIKES:** Being trapped in jars
**THREAT RATING:** LOW
**APPEARS IN:** 130

# Really Hungry Caterpillar

A tiny caterpillar with an enormous appetite who witnessed Mr Big Nose being kidnapped by vegetables and later travelled to the Vegetable Kingdom with Terry and me.

**SUPER POWER:** Ability to eat anything, including flying fried-egg cars, steamrollers, rhinoceroses, wacky waving inflatable arm-flailing tube men and giant mutant spiders
**LIKES:** Eating
**DISLIKES:** Birds
**THREAT RATING:** EXTREME
**APPEARS IN:** 52

Hello!

Hello!

# RUDOLPH THE RED-NOSED REINDEER

**Santa's most famous reindeer, known for his glowing red nose that helps guide Santa's sleigh through the sky at night.**

**SUPER POWER:** Glowing red nose
**LIKES:** Playing reindeer games with Dasher, Dancer, Prancer, Vixen, Comet, Cupid, Donner and Blitzen
**DISLIKES:** Being left out of reindeer games
**THREAT RATING:** LOW
**APPEARS IN:** 156

# SANTA

**Plump man with a long white beard who, one night a year, leaves his home in the North Pole and flies around the world in a sleigh pulled by reindeer to deliver presents to children who celebrate Christmas.**

**SUPER POWER:** Ability to travel around the world in one night
**LIKES:** Children, milk, cookies, reindeer
**DISLIKES:** Narrow chimneys, unexpected puddles
**THREAT RATING:** LOW
**APPEARS IN:** 156

Giraffe noise.

# Silky & Friends

Silky is Jill's favourite pet. She was a regular cat until Terry painted her canary-yellow and launched her from the treehouse, whereupon she grew wings, became a catnary and made friends with twelve other flying cats.

1

**SILKY**

2 **PUFFY**

3 **PURRY**

4 **BLURRY**

5 **SCARY**

6 **FAIRY**

7 **SCRATCHY**

8 **SLASHY**

9 **TRASHY**

10 **FLUFFY**

11 **CRASHY**

12 **TINKERBELL**

13 **FLOPPY**

Hello!

WHO'S WHO

Hello!

**SUPER POWER:** Being able to fly
**LIKES:** Cat food, cuddles, cats on TV, flying
**DISLIKES:** Dogs, water, fleas, locked cat flaps, giant gorillas
**THREAT RATING:** LOW, unless you are a giant gorilla
**APPEARS IN:** All books

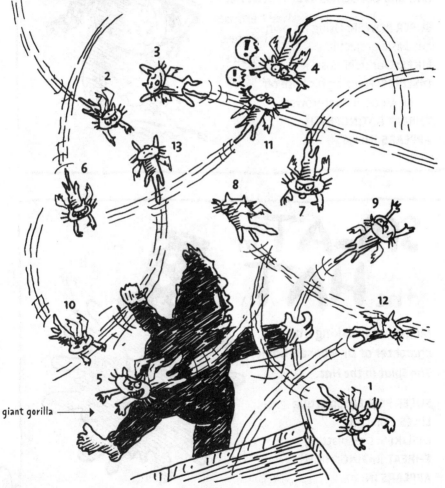

giant gorilla →

# Snowman

A not-very-Christmassy snowman who tricked Terry and me into making him one Christmas Eve.

**SUPER POWER:** Using his own head as a projectile
**LIKES:** Our treehouse
**DISLIKES:** Freezing his base off in the Arctic, flamethrowers
**THREAT RATING:** HIGH
**APPEARS IN:** 156

# SPLAT in the HAT

← hat

splat ↓

Mega mess-making main character of Dr Moose's book *The Splat in the Hat*.

**SUPER POWER:** Splatting
**LIKES:** Splatting
**DISLIKES:** De-splatting
**THREAT RATING:** HIGH
**APPEARS IN:** 117

Hello!

Hello!

# SPY COWS

Cows that spied on the treehouse while *Treehouse: The Movie* was being made. They stole all our ideas and made *Cowhouse: The Mooo-vie*.

**SUPER POWER:** Sneaking around stealing movie ideas
**LIKES:** Spying and stealing
**DISLIKES:** Coming up with their own ideas
**THREAT RATING:** HIGH, if you have ideas you don't want stolen
**APPEAR IN:** 78

# *Story* POLICE

Police force dedicated to stamping out bad storytelling.

**SUPER POWER:** Ability to detect clichés and plot holes
**LIKES:** Good writing
**DISLIKES:** Bad writing featuring outlandish plots, ridiculous characters, silly names, needless repetition (i.e. needless repetition), time-wasting chases and clichéd endings (e.g. it was all a dream)
**THREAT RATING:** HIGH, especially if you're Terry and me
**APPEAR IN:** 117

## Super BW

After time-travelling with Terry and me, the safety inspector Inspector Bubblewrap discovered his inner risk-taker, became a stuntman and changed his name to Super BW.

bubblewrap cape

**SUPER POWER:** Jumping his motorcycle over long distances
**LIKES:** Adventure
**DISLIKES:** Being overly cautious
**THREAT RATING:** LOW
**APPEARS IN:** 65

## SUPERFINGER

Superfinger is no ordinary finger. Superfinger is a superhero who solves problems requiring finger-based solutions.

**SUPER POWER:** Providing finger-based solutions to finger-based problems
**LIKES:** His sidekick Pinky and Jimi Handrix
**DISLIKES:** Blocked noses
**THREAT RATING:** HIGH, but only if you are causing a problem that requires a finger-based solution
**APPEARS IN:** 13, 39

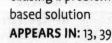

Hello!

Hello!

# TERRIBLE-TERRY

Terry's mischief-making doppelganger who dwells in the doppelganger mirror with his mirror gang pals Anti-Andy and Junkyard-Jill.

**SUPER POWER:** Being terrible
**LIKES:** Mischief-making
**DISLIKES:** Monkeys
**THREAT RATING:** LOW
**APPEARS IN:** 169

# TERRY

pencil →

**This is my friend Terry. He lives in the treehouse with me and draws all the pictures for the books.**

**SUPER POWER:** Drawing, inventing
**LIKES:** Drawing; reading; playing with penguins; dreaming; inventing gadgets, gizmos and machines
**DISLIKES:** Monkeys, pirates, vegetables, being shouted at by our publisher Mr Big Nose
**THREAT RATING:** LOW, unless you're a monkey because he really hates monkeys
**APPEARS IN:** All books

Giraffe noise.

# TERRY'S PARENTS

Terry's danger-obsessed parents tried to protect him from every possible danger in the world. They even had Terry fitted with emergency self-inflating underpants so he'd be safe if he ever fell into water.

**SUPER POWER:** Being able to see danger everywhere
**LIKES:** Alarms, helmets, seatbelts, padded rooms
**DISLIKES:** Danger
**THREAT RATING:** LOW
**APPEAR IN:** 26

Terry

emergency self-inflating underpants

parents

# THREE WISE OWLS

Three owls that live in the treehouse and shout random words. We don't always know what they mean, but that's because they're *so* wise.

**SUPER POWER:** SHOUTING!
**LIKES:** MICE! MICE! MICE!
**DISLIKES:** AARDVARKS! CHEESE STICKS! POOP-POOP!
**THREAT RATING:** LOW
**APPEAR IN:** 65, 104, 143

AARDVARK!

CHEESE STICKS!!

POOP-POOP!!!

Hello!

Hello!

# TOOTH FAIRY

fairy wand

fairy wings

A tiny magical tooth-disposal expert who, along with her tooth fairy helpers, visited the treehouse and exchanged my old tooth for the golden coin that I needed to buy a Joke Writer 2000™.

**SUPER POWER:** Tooth collecting, tooth disposal
**LIKES:** Collecting and disposing of teeth
**DISLIKES:** False teeth
**THREAT RATING:** LOW
**APPEARS IN:** 104

fairy feet

# Tooth Fairy Helpers

Achey, Molar, Driller and Smash are the key members of the tooth fairy's tooth-collection team.

**SUPER POWER:** Tooth collecting
**LIKES:** Collecting teeth
**DISLIKES:** Having to wait for children to go to sleep before they can start work
**THREAT RATING:** LOW
**APPEAR IN:** 104

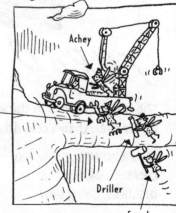

Achey

Molar

Driller

Smash

Giraffe noise.

# The TRUNKINATOR

A boxing elephant who lives in the treehouse. Generally peaceful but can knock a person out with just one punch from his mighty trunk if challenged.

PAF!

**SUPER POWER:** The ability to trunk-punch
**LIKES:** Boxing, spending time with friends, knitting
**DISLIKES:** Professor Stupido (who once un-invented him)
**THREAT RATING:** EXTREME, in the boxing ring; LOW, outside the boxing ring
**APPEARS IN:** 39, 91, 104, 117, 143

A turbo tortoise →

VAROOM!

# TURBO TORTOISE

The fastest animal in the whole animal kingdom—faster even than a cow driving a red Ferrari!

**SUPER POWER:** Going fast
**LIKES:** Going fast
**DISLIKES:** Going slow

**THREAT RATING:** LOW, unless you're in its way when it's going fast
**APPEARS IN:** 78

Hello!

Hello!

# Vegetable Patty

Vegetable fighter on a life-long quest to rid the world of vegetables in order to avenge the death of her parents, who were crushed by giant vegetables at a farmers' market.

**SUPER POWER:** Vegetable-fighting skills
**LIKES:** Boiling, broiling, crunching, munching, knock-out punching, grabbing, stabbing and shish kebabbing vegetables
**DISLIKES:** Vegetables
**THREAT RATING:** EXTREME, if you are a vegetable
**APPEARS IN:** 52

# VERY ANGRY DUCK

The final—and most important—part of the defence system in my high-security potato chip storage facility. You don't want to mess with this very angry duck ... so don't try to steal my chips!

**SUPER POWER:** Anger
**LIKES:** Quacking and fighting
**DISLIKES:** Chip thieves
**THREAT RATING:** HIGH
**APPEARS IN:** 78

QUACK!

Giraffe noise.

## WACKY WAVING INFLATABLE ARM-FLAILING TUBE MEN

Fun-loving, attention-grabbing inflatable tube men who love to wave their arms in the air like they just don't care and dance like nobody is watching all day long.

**SUPER POWER:** Attracting attention
**LIKES:** Wildly waving their arms and jerking their upper bodies in unpredictable directions
**DISLIKES:** Sharp objects and really hungry caterpillars
**THREAT RATING:** LOW
**APPEAR IN:** 52

pen

notepad

## WANDA write-a-lot

Writes articles for *Go Away!* travel magazine and visited the treehouse with photographer Jimmy Snapshot to do a story on our camping holiday.

**SUPER POWER:** Curiosity
**LIKES:** Asking questions
**DISLIKES:** Anyone or anything that won't answer her questions
**THREAT RATING:** LOW
**APPEARS IN:** 143, 169

Hello!

Hello!

# YOU, THE READER

You, i.e. the reader, i.e. the person taking in the sense or meaning of the letters, symbols and pictures contained in our books, i.e. reading.

**SUPER POWER:** Decoding letters, symbols and pictures
**LIKES:** Reading, listening
**DISLIKES:** Waiting for the next book to be written
**THREAT RATING:** LOW
**APPEAR IN:** All books

Giraffe noise.

ALL the CHARACTERS

# PART TWO

# WHAT'S WHERE

## ALL the LEVELS

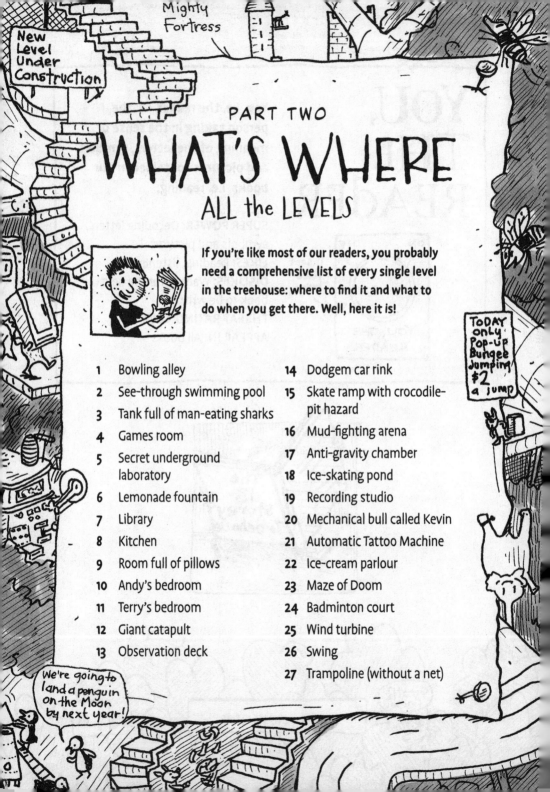

If you're like most of our readers, you probably need a comprehensive list of every single level in the treehouse: where to find it and what to do when you get there. Well, here it is!

1 Bowling alley

2 See-through swimming pool

3 Tank full of man-eating sharks

4 Games room

5 Secret underground laboratory

6 Lemonade fountain

7 Library

8 Kitchen

9 Room full of pillows

10 Andy's bedroom

11 Terry's bedroom

12 Giant catapult

13 Observation deck

14 Dodgem car rink

15 Skate ramp with crocodile-pit hazard

16 Mud-fighting arena

17 Anti-gravity chamber

18 Ice-skating pond

19 Recording studio

20 Mechanical bull called Kevin

21 Automatic Tattoo Machine

22 Ice-cream parlour

23 Maze of Doom

24 Badminton court

25 Wind turbine

26 Swing

27 Trampoline (without a net)

Mighty Fortress

New Level Under Construction

TODAY only Pop-Up Bungee Jumping $2 a jump

We're going to land a penguin on the Moon by next year!

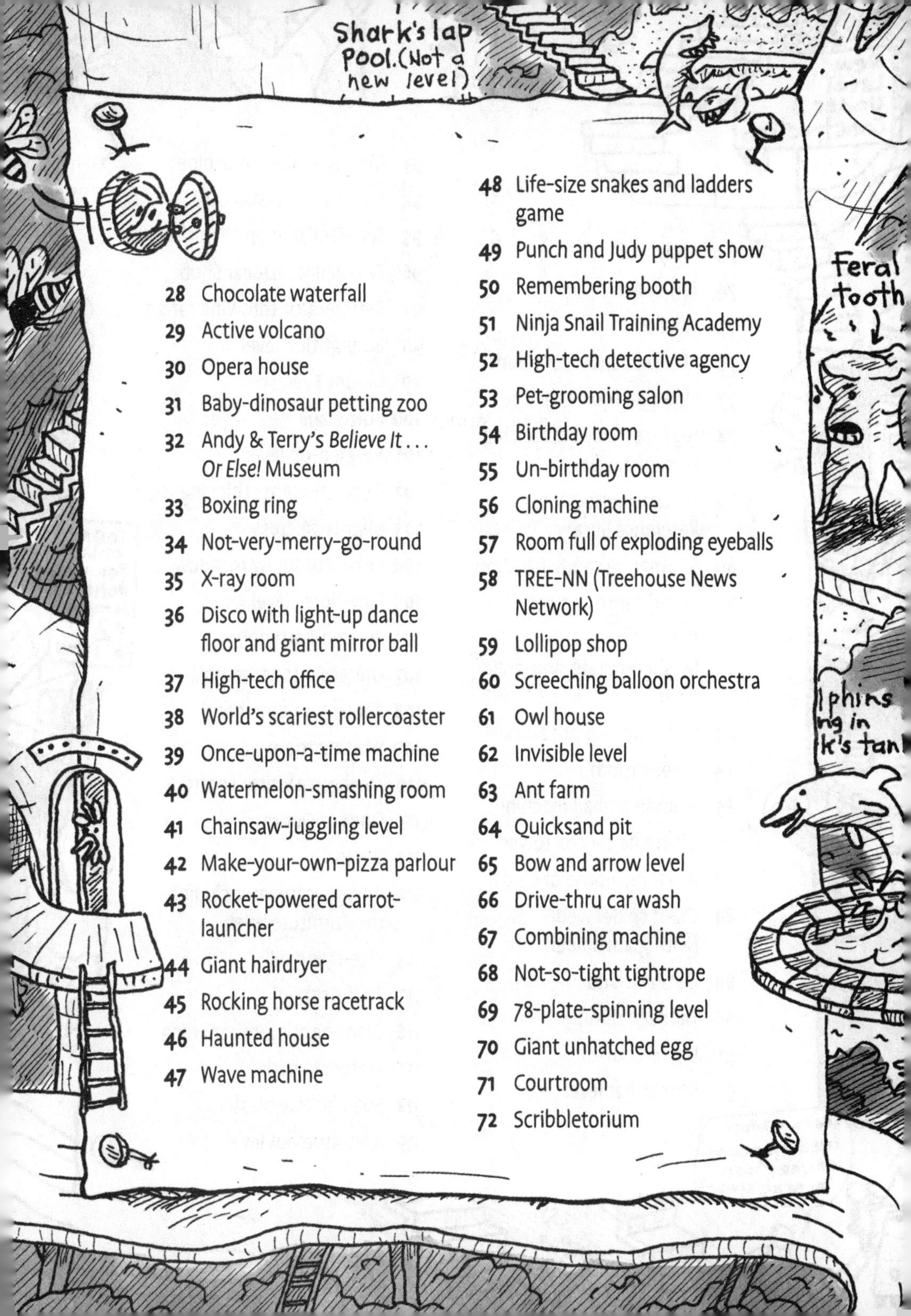

Shark's lap pool. (Not a new level)

Feral tooth

lphins
ng in
k's tan

Mighty Fortress

New Level Under Construction

73 Andyland
74 Terrytown
75 Jillville
76 ALL-BALL sports stadium
77 Open-air movie theatre
78 High-security potato chip storage facility
79 Fortune-telling tent/ Reference library
80 Submarine sandwich shop
81 World's most powerful whirlpool
82 Mashed-potato-and-gravy train
83 Spin-and-win prize wheel
84 Trophy room
85 Human pinball machine
86 Air-traffic control tower
87 91-storey house of cards
88 Giant spider web (with giant spider)
89 Desert island
90 Garbage dump
91 Big red button
92 Stupid-hat level

93 Money-making machine
94 Never-ending staircase
95 Two-Dollar Shop
96 Two-Million-Dollar Shop
97 Refrigerator-throwing range
98 Bunfighting level
99 Mount Everest
100 Burp bank
101 Tangled-up level
102 Deep-thoughts thinking room
103 Mighty fortress
104 Beautiful sunny meadow
105 Tiny-horse level
106 Pyjama-party room
107 Underpants Museum
108 Photo-bombing booth
109 Waiting room
110 Treehouse visitor centre
111 Door of Doom
112 Circus
113 All-you-can-eat-including-the-furniture level
114 Kite-flying hill
115 Traffic school
116 Giant-fighting-robot arena
117 Water-ski park
118 Soap bubble blaster
119 Non-stop dot level

TODAY ONLY Pop-up Bungee Jumping $2 a jump

We're going to land a penguin on the Moon by next year!

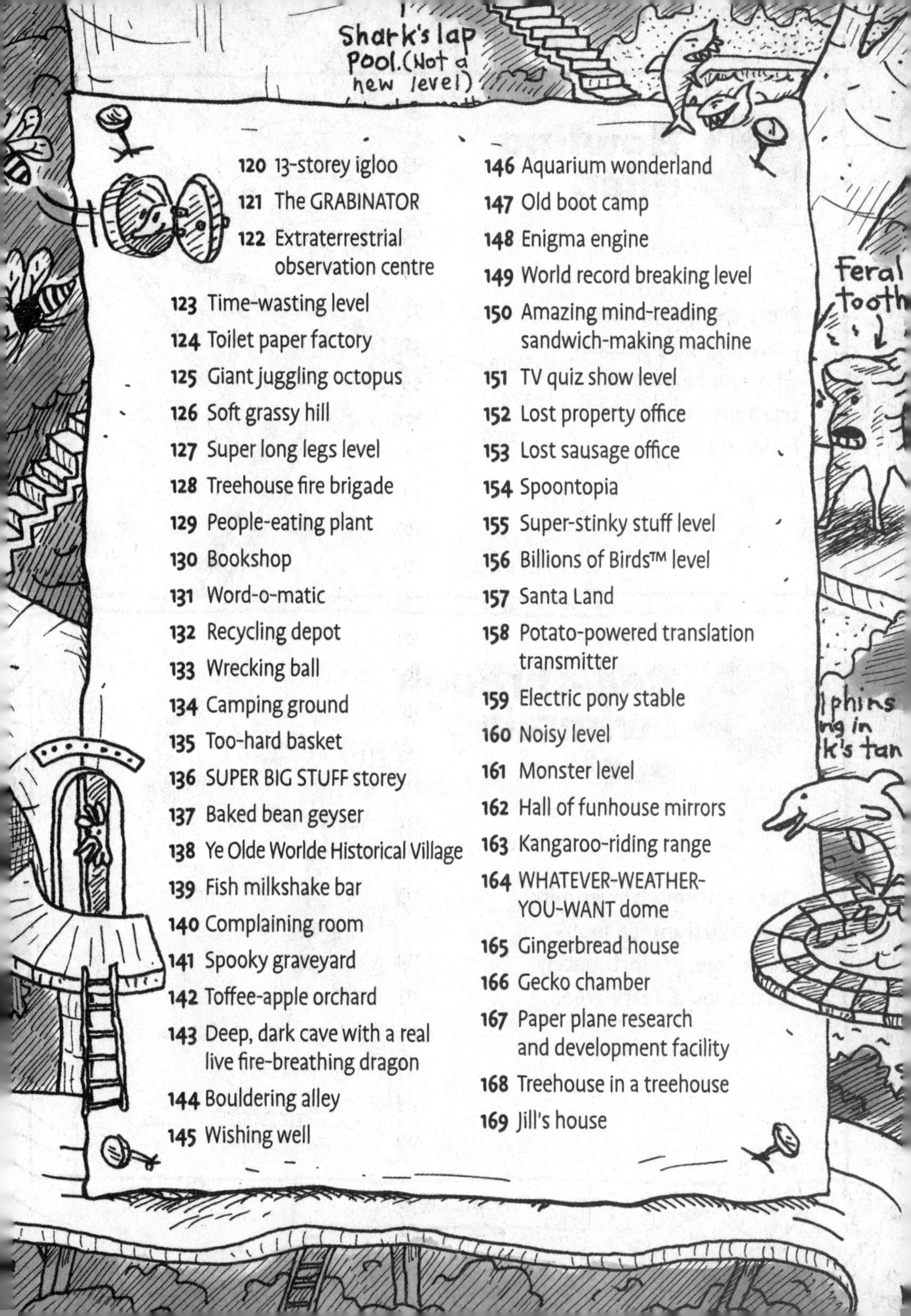

Shark's lap pool. (Not a new level)

Feral tooth

lphins ng in k's tan

# 1 Bowling alley

Every treehouse needs a bowling alley because who ever heard of a treehouse without a bowling alley?

# 2 See-through swimming pool

Our see-through swimming pool is guaranteed 100% shark-free. (Unfortunately it's not 100% Terry-free.)

WHAT'S WHERE

## 3

# Tank full of man-eating sharks

Man-eating* sharks are a lot of fun, but you do have to be careful, especially when feeding them.

*MAN-EATING SHARKS DON'T ONLY EAT MEN—THEY WILL EAT PEOPLE OF ALL GENDERS AND AGES, AS WELL AS FISH, PIRATES AND TERRY'S UNDERPANTS.

## 4

# Games room

A state-of-the-art games room—we guarantee you won't have any more fun anywhere on the entire planet* than here!

* MANY PLACES EXCLUDED.

## 5 Secret* underground laboratory

This is where we invent a lot of really cool stuff, like banana enlargers, marshmallow machines, vegetable vaporisers and super-duper sucker-upperers.

* OKAY, OBVIOUSLY IT'S NOT COMPLETELY SECRET BECAUSE WE JUST TOLD YOU ABOUT IT, BUT PLEASE DON'T TELL ANYONE ELSE.

## 6 Lemonade fountain

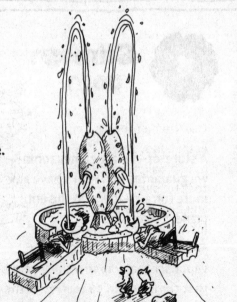

It's just like a regular fountain, but instead of water it has lemonade. You can have any flavour you want as long as it's red, orange, lemon, cola or tutti-frutti (which is all the flavours mixed together).

WHAT'S WHERE

# 7 Library

This is where we keep all our
favourite books*—including the ones we write.

\* MY FAVOURITE BOOK IS *THE MAGIC FARAWAY TREE*, TERRY'S
IS *TREASURE ISLAND* AND JILL'S IS *THE STORY OF FERDINAND*.

# 8 Kitchen

Our kitchen comes
equipped with a
marshmallow machine
that follows you around
and fires marshmallows
into your mouth whenever
you're hungry and a vegetable
vaporiser that vaporises any vegetables
that come within 50 metres of the treehouse.

# Room full of pillows

**9**

It's a room full of pillows*.
You know how pillows work.
It's not *that* complicated.

Room
full of
pillows

\* THIS IS THE SOFTEST—AND
SAFEST—ROOM IN THE TREEHOUSE.

# Andy's bedroom

**10**

This is where I sleep*. It's the best bedroom
in the treehouse, no question.

Andy's ↑
Bedroom

\* WHICH IS HARDLY
EVER BECAUSE WHO'S
GOT TIME TO SLEEP
WHEN THERE'S SO
MUCH FUN TO BE HAD?

WHAT'S WHERE

# Terry's bedroom

Terry's Bedroom

This is where Terry sleeps. It's the worst* bedroom in the treehouse, no question.

\* TERRY LEAVES A LOT OF STINKY SOCKS LYING AROUND. (GAS MASK RECOMMENDED.)

# Giant catapult

Giant Catapult

Great for getting rid of monkeys, pirates and other unwanted guests. (I also like to put Terry in there when he's asleep and fling him out of the tree. Yeah, I know, I don't really have to go to all that trouble, but what are friends for?)

ALL the LEVELS

73

## Observation deck

Our observation deck features a long-range telescope that allows us to see everything that's going on pretty much everywhere.

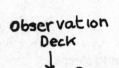

Observation
Deck
↓

 ## Dodgem car rink

Dodgem cars are fun, sure, but dodgem cars high up in a tree are even more fun. (And at our rink there is a NO No Bumping rule!)

PUTT PUTT PUTT

SMASH!

CRASH!

WHAT'S WHERE

## 15 Skate ramp with crocodile-pit hazard

Skateboarding over a crocodile pit full of live crocodiles can be hazardous, so it's not recommended for beginners. (Or Terry.)

## 16 Mud-fighting arena

The only thing more enjoyable than a good mud fight is watching one from the comfort of our purpose-built mud-fighting arena.

## 17 Anti-gravity chamber

Floating is the next best thing to flying, and our anti-gravity chamber is the perfect—and safest—place to do it because there's no risk of floating away into the sky and never being seen again. (We do, however, recommend that you empty your pockets of all valuables before floating.)

## 18 Ice-skating pond

Originally intended for Terry, Jill and me to skate on but it was quickly adopted as home by a colony of ice-skating penguins.

# 19 Recording studio

This is where we have written and recorded all of our number-one smash hit songs, including 'Tinkle, Tinkle, Little Terry', 'Rock Around the Treehouse', 'Hey Jill' and 'Never-ending Staircase to Heaven'.

# 20 Mechanical bull called Kevin

Okay, I admit it, we only called the bull Kevin so it would rhyme with 'seven' in the ten unlucky pirates rhyme (see *The 26-Storey Treehouse*). Its actual name is Algernon (which doesn't rhyme with anything).

## 21 Automatic Tattoo Machine

If you want a tattoo but can't decide on a design, just relax and let the ATM decide for you!

## 22 Ice-cream parlour

Our ice-cream parlour is run by Edward Scooperhands and there are 78 flavours to choose from, including rocky road, winding road and, my favourite, dirt road!

WHAT'S WHERE

## 23 Maze of Doom

A maze so complicated that no one who's gone in has ever come out again*.

* EXCEPT FOR TERRY, JILL, CAPTAIN WOODENHEAD AND ME.

Stupid GPS!

## 24 Badminton court

I don't know why they call it BADminton when it's so GOOD to play!

## 25 Wind turbine

Our treehouse runs on 100% fully renewable wind power thanks to our wind turbine. (On days when there's not enough wind we just set up our giant hairdryer to power it for us.)

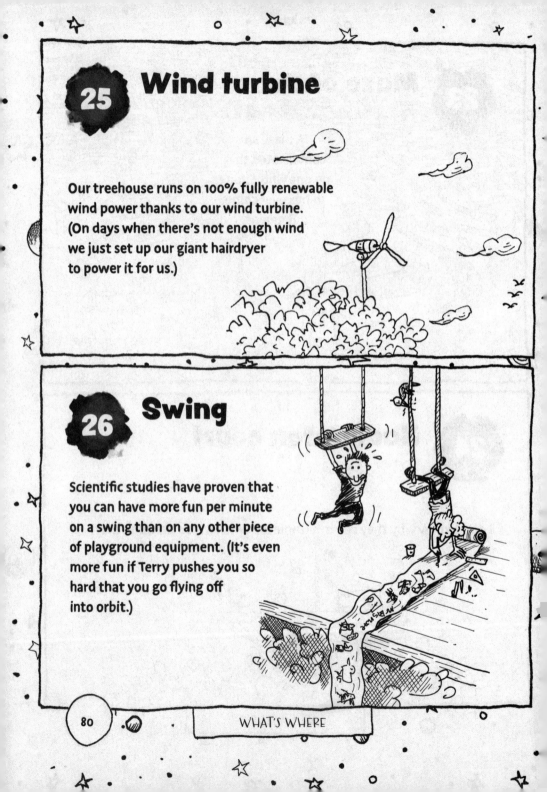

## 26 Swing

Scientific studies have proven that you can have more fun per minute on a swing than on any other piece of playground equipment. (It's even more fun if Terry pushes you so hard that you go flying off into orbit.)

# Trampoline (without a net)

If you're going to put a trampoline in a treehouse the best place is at the very top so there are no branches above you to crash into. It also allows you to wave to the pilots and passengers of passing planes.

# Chocolate waterfall

This is our favourite place to not *not* swim in the treehouse. It's hot chocolate, too, so you can spend all day and all night in there (and we often do!).

## 29 Active volcano

This volcano is great for toasting marshmallows, Terry. Are you sure it's not going to erupt?

Relax, Andy, of course, I'm sure.

Marshmallows are good, campfire-toasted marshmallows are even better, but volcano-toasted marshmallows are the best!

## 30 Opera house

Okay, so it's not *the* Sydney Opera House— it's a replica, but it's such a good copy that it's even more like the opera house than the original.

JIMI HANDRIX AND SUPERFINGER JAMMING HERE TONIGHT AND EVERY NIGHT

WHAT'S WHERE

# 31 Baby-dinosaur petting zoo

Many people are terrified of dinosaurs—and for good reason—but baby dinosaurs are surprisingly cute.

NOTE: DO, HOWEVER, KEEP YOUR FINGERS AWAY FROM THEIR MOUTHS, WHICH, WHILE SMALL, CONTAIN MANY EXTREMELY SHARP TEETH.

# 32 Andy & Terry's *Believe It ... or Else!* Museum

You'd better believe that everything we have on display here is 100% genuine ... OR ELSE*!

* WE HAVEN'T FIGURED OUT WHAT THE 'OR ELSE' BIT IS YET BECAUSE EVERYBODY WHO'S VISITED SO FAR HAS BELIEVED EVERYTHING, BUT YOU'D BETTER BELIEVE THAT WHATEVER THE 'OR ELSE' IS, YOU'RE NOT GOING TO LIKE IT!

ALL the LEVELS

## **Boxing ring**

**33**

Our boxing ring comes complete with a boxing elephant called The Trunkinator, who many visitors are surprised to learn is actually a peaceful creature who will only box if challenged*.

\* WARNING: THE TRUNKINATOR REMAINS UNDEFEATED, EXCEPT FOR HIS RUN-IN WITH MR BIG NOSE'S GRANDCHILDREN, ALICE, ALBERT AND THE BABY.

PAF!

Roll up, roll up...
Try your luck with
the **TRUNKINATOR!**

## **Not-very-merry-go-round**

**34**

AAARRRRRGGHHH!!

No matter how tightly you hold on, you will fly off the not-very-merry-go-round— it's impossible not to.

WHAT'S WHERE

## 35 X-ray room

Of all the rays there are, X-rays are definitely the X-rayiest! They can help you see everything, even your own skeleton!

YIKES! A SKELETON.

Relax, Terry. It's yours.

Nooo..! I've got a SKELETON inside me!!!

## 36 Disco with light-up dance floor and giant mirror ball

One of the most popular levels in the treehouse, as you can see by how crowded it is.

# High-tech office

Laser-eraser

Semi-automatic staple gun

Jet-propelled swivel chair

Laser-eraser

Semi-automatic staple gun

Jet-propelled swivel chair

Our high-tech office is equipped with laser-erasers, jet-propelled swivel chairs and semi-automatic staple guns. Great for settling workplace disputes or just messing around while you're supposed to be working*.

* WHICH I MUST ADMIT IS DIFFICULT WHEN YOU HAVE A HIGH-TECH OFFICE AS MUCH FUN AS THIS.

# 38 World's scariest rollercoaster

A rollercoaster ride so fast, so dangerous and so terrifying that even dead people are too scared to go on it.

ARGHHH!?

EEEEEKK!?

Nooo!

I dare you to have a ride

No way! I may be dead, but I'm not crazy!

YOU HAVE TO BE THIS BIG TO RIDE

ONLY FOR THE VERY BRAVE

FRIGHTENING

VERY DEADLY

DANGER SCARY

## 39 Once-upon-a-time machine

A writing and drawing machine that has many hands, including one pair for typing at super speed and another pair for drawing. It can write and draw a book of any length and in any genre according to your exact specifications (see pages 88–89 for more details).

NOTE: AFTER THIS MACHINE WAS STOLEN TERRY BUILT AN EGG TIMER AND A WHEELIE BIN TIME MACHINE ON THIS LEVEL (SEE PAGES 184 & 197).

## 40 Watermelon-smashing room

A purpose-built watermelon-smashing facility dedicated to the not-so-gentle art of watermelon smashing. It's everything a watermelon-smashing enthusiast could wish for.

# THE ONCE-UPON-A-TIME MACHINE: How it works

You can program the Once-upon-a-time machine to write the exact story you would write if you weren't too busy doing other things. So set, forget and GO HAVE SOME FUN!!!

How funny do you want
your story to be?

How much action?

You'll need characters: choose as many—or as few—as you want!

WHAT'S WHERE

How much—or how little—romance?

## Romance dial

What challenges will your characters face?

## Disaster dial

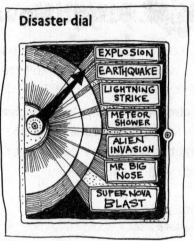

Where will your story be set?

## Settings menu

How long—or how short—will your story be?

## Pagelengthometer

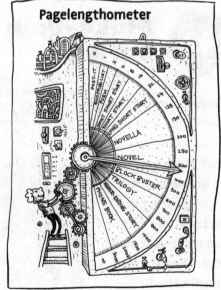

How will your characters get around?

## Fruit- and vegetable-based transport options

# 41 Chainsaw-juggling level

Chainsaws don't juggle themselves, you know, so someone has to do it. Might as well be us . . . and maybe even you!

NOTE: BYO SPARE EARS, NOSES, FINGERS ETC.

# 42 Make-your-own-pizza parlour

If you like extra snails, choc chips and/or fresh cactus spikes on your pizza, well that's no problem. In our make-your-own-pizza parlour you can make your own pizzas just the way you like them!

WHAT'S WHERE

## 43 Rocket-powered carrot-launcher

This is the ultimate in long-range carrot-launching technology. Your carrots will never again fall short of their targets.

Check! Check! Double check!

Such a waste

Criminal.

I'm hungry.

Sob!

## 44 Giant hairdryer

Our giant hairdryer is so strong it practically blasts the hair right off your head. Dries—or removes—your hair in record time.

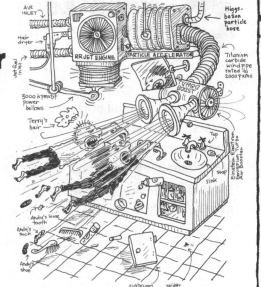

AIR INLET

Higgs-boson particle hose

Hair dryer

RRJET ENGINE

PARTICLE ACCELERATOR

Titanium carbide windpipe rated to 2000 pxiho

Jet fuel inlet

3000 kpmxbf power bellows

TURBO BOOST

Terry's hair

Tap

Einstein Electron Emission Turbo Air Booster

soap

sink

Andy's loose tooth

Andy's sock

Andy's shoe

cupboard door

spider

# Rocking horse racetrack

Rocking horses and rocking horse racetracks rock, right?!

# Haunted house

Guaranteed to be full of ghostly ghosts, brain-eating zombies, giant spiders, rabid rats, blood-thirsty vampires and hideous hobyahs . . . or your money/life back!

WHAT'S WHERE

# 47 Wave machine

Why bother going to the beach when you can surf a giant wave any time you like in the convenience of your own treehouse?

# 48 Life-size snakes and ladders game

This snakes and ladders game has real snakes and real ladders—what's not to like (unless you don't like real snakes and/or real ladders)?

## 49 Punch and Judy puppet show

This puppet show runs 24-hours a day, 7 days a week and is a lot of fun, as long as you don't stand too close to the stage.

## 50 Remembering booth

Our remembering booth is perfect for remembering all the things you've ever forgotten, even the things you've forgotten that you've forgotten.

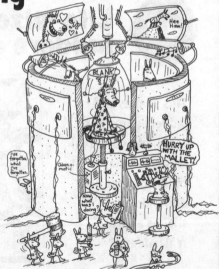

## 51 Ninja Snail Training Academy

The greatest— and only—Ninja Snail Training Academy in the world.

## 52 High-tech detective agency

Our detective agency has all the latest high-tech detective technology, including a complete set of magnifying glasses, a hot-donut vending machine and a Disguise-o-matic 5000*, which has a disguise for every occasion!

\* SEE FOLLOWING PAGE FOR DETAILS.

# THE DISGUISE-O-MATIC 5000:
## How it works

You'll never be without the exact disguise you need with the Disguise-o-matic 5000. Our Disguise-o-matic 5000 comes equipped with 5000 different disguises. That's more than most people will need in a lifetime: a completely different disguise every single day for at least thirteen years! You can disguise yourself as anything:

An old man . . .

a frogpotamus . . .

a street sign . . .

WHAT'S WHERE

a horse . . .

a piece of broccoli . . . a carrot . . . or even a cob of corn!

You don't ever have to be yourself again with the Disguise-o-matic 5000!

## Pet-grooming salon

Jill runs our pet-grooming salon because the only thing she loves more than animals is washing, cutting and styling their fur.

## Birthday room

It's always your birthday in the birthday room, even when it's not. You can have a birthday party as many times a year/month/week/day as you like!

WHAT'S WHERE

## 55 Un-birthday room

Every time you enter this room you lose a birthday. The more times you go in, the younger you get!

## 56 Cloning machine

The cloning machine makes perfect clones of you and your friends—as many as you need!

NOTE: DON'T LET TERRY MAKE HUNDREDS OF TERRY CLONES . . . THEY'RE REALLY ANNOYING!

## 57 Room full of exploding eyeballs

Look, I'm going to be completely honest here—I don't even know why we invented this level. I mean, who would want their eyeballs to explode*?

\* LOTS OF PEOPLE, JUDGING BY HOW POPULAR THIS LEVEL IS WITH OUR VISITORS. GO FIGURE!

## 58 TREE-NN (Treehouse News Network)

A 24-hour TV news centre, featuring regular updates on all the latest treehouse news, current affairs and gossip.

WHAT'S WHERE

## 59 Lollipop shop

Mary Lollipoppins, the lollipop-serving robot, not only serves the best lollipops from the past and the present, she also serves lollipops from the future!

One of those and two of those and one of those and three of those and four of those and five of those and...

## 60 Screeching balloon orchestra

You know when you pinch the end of a balloon and let the air out slowly to make an annoying screeching sound? Well, this orchestra takes it to the next level.

SCREECH!!

# Owl house

The three wise owls who live in our owl house are the wisest owls in the treehouse. (Which is not saying much because they're the *only* owls in the treehouse.)

AARDVARK!

CHEESE STICKS!!

POOP. POOP!!!

They're so wise!

# Invisible level

Everything—and everyone— is invisible in the invisible level— even you!

Terry, where are you?

I don't know!

WHAT'S WHERE

# 63 Ant farm

Sixty-five chambers of non-stop, 24/7, around-the-clock, ant-packed action!

# 64 Quicksand pit

Quicksand is the coolest sort of sand there is . . . unless you're sinking in it, in which case it's not quite so cool, although that being said, it's still pretty cool.

## 65 Bow and arrow level

Unlike normal archery ranges, there are no rules here. You can fire your arrows at whatever—and whoever—you like*!

* BUT PLEASE TRY TO AVOID ME.
(THAT MEANS YOU, TERRY!)

## 66 Drive-thru car wash

There are few things that are as much fun, or as wet, as driving through a drive-thru car wash with the top open and your windows down!

WHAT'S WHERE

## 67 Combining machine

This machine allows you to combine any thing with any other thing—animal, vegetable or mineral: the choice is yours.

## 68 Not-so-tight tightrope

It's much harder than you think to make tightropes tight . . . so we don't even try.

## 69 78-plate-spinning level

Can you get all 78 plates spinning—and keep them spinning forever and ever and ever? If so, please come quickly because we're exhausted!

## 70 Giant unhatched egg

We don't know where it came from, but there's only one thing to do when you find a giant unhatched egg in your treehouse: sit on it and see what comes out!

## 71 Courtroom

Our courtroom is run by a robot judge called Edward Gavelhead, who uses his gavel-shaped head as a gavel.

## 72 Scribbletorium

Scribble up a storm in our Scribbletorium. You can scribble on the walls, the floors, the roof and even yourself!

## 73 Andyland

Andyland is the land where we put all the Andy clones that we created in the cloning machine. (It's the Andy-est place on Earth and my favourite level in the whole treehouse!)

## 74 Terrytown

Terrytown is the town where we put all the Terry clones that we created in the cloning machine. (This is the most Terryible place on Earth and Terry's favourite level in the whole treehouse!)

WHAT'S WHERE

## 75 Jillville

This is the village where we put all the Jill clones that we created in the cloning machine. (And, yes, you guessed it, this is the silliest—I mean Jilliest—place on Earth and Jill's favourite level in the whole treehouse!)

## 76 ALL-BALL sports stadium

Play all ball sports all at the same time—basketball, football (all codes), baseball, volleyball, speedball, dodgeball, handball and even fireball!

ALL the LEVELS

# 77 Open-air movie theatre

Our open-air movie theatre has a super-giant screen and we also serve super-giant popcorn/popfish* in super-giant popcorn/popfish boxes.

* FOR THE PENGUINS.

# 78 High-security potato chip storage facility

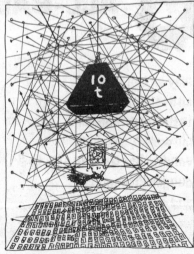

My high-security potato chip safe is protected by 1000 loaded mousetraps, 100 laser beams, a 10-tonne weight and a very angry duck*.

* SO DON'T TRY TO STEAL MY CHIPS, OR ELSE!

## 79 Fortune-telling tent/ Reference library

We let fortune teller Madam Know-it-all set up her tent in our treehouse, but if we'd been able to see into the future we would have known that this was not a good idea.

NOTE: LATER, AFTER MADAM KNOW-IT-ALL'S UNFORTUNATE ACCIDENT—AND REALISING THAT BOOKS ARE A MUCH BETTER SOURCE OF INFORMATION THAN FORTUNE TELLERS—WE CHANGED THIS LEVEL TO THE MADAM KNOW-IT-ALL MEMORIAL REFERENCE LIBRARY.

## 80 Submarine sandwich shop

Our submarine sandwich shop is the only submarine sandwich shop in the world that sells sandwiches the size of actual submarines!

NOTE: NEVER EAT THE SUBMARINE SANDWICH THAT YOU ARE TRAVELLING IN.

## 81 World's most powerful whirlpool

There are many safe places to swim in the treehouse: the see-through-swimming pool, the chocolate waterfall and the bath, just to name a few. The world's most dangerous whirlpool is not one of them.

## 82 Mashed-potato-and-gravy train

All aboard the mashed-potato-and-gravy train! Stopping all stations to Mashed Potato and Gravy Heaven!

## 83 Spin-and-win prize wheel

What will you win? A trip to Mars or a poke in the eye? One million dollars or a kick in the pants? You'll never know unless you spin!

## 84 Trophy room

We've won a lot of trophies over the years—so many, in fact, that we had to create an entire room to keep them all in. (And, yes, there's a trophy for having the most trophies in a trophy room—we have one of those, too.)

## 85 Human pinball machine

The only thing more fun than playing pinball on a pinball machine is getting to be the pinball yourself!

## 86 Air-traffic control tower

Controlling air-traffic is a highly skilled job on which the lives of hundreds of thousands of air-travellers depend every hour. Luckily, we have an air-traffic control tower to ensure everyone stays safe!

WHAT'S WHERE

## 87 91-storey house of cards

Shhh . . . be quiet . . .
don't run . . . don't jump . . .
don't breathe . . . and
whatever else you don't do,
DON'T TURN ON THE FAN!

## 88 Giant spider web (with giant spider)

We thought having a giant spider
web with a giant spider in it was
a good idea. We were wrong*.

* VERY WRONG!

# 89 Desert island

There's nothing like a remote desert island for getting away from it all. Fortunately, we have one right in our treehouse so we can get away and then get right back to it all in no time.

# 90 Garbage dump

The best thing about our garbage dump is that is has an old wardrobe on top that is the entrance to the magical world of Banarnia*.

* BANARNIA IS JUST LIKE NARNIA, EXCEPT NOTHING LIKE NARNIA AT ALL REALLY (APART FROM ENTERING IT THROUGH A WARDROBE). (SEE PAGE 162 FOR MORE INFORMATION.)

# 91 Big red button

Our big red button is the biggest and reddest big red button you've ever seen. Unfortunately, we're never sure whether to push it or not because we can never quite remember what it does.

# 92 Stupid-hat level

If you think regular hats are stupid, wait till you see the stupid hats on our stupid-hat level—they're the stupidest stupid hats in the world!

## 93 Money-making machine

Our money-making machine not only makes money, it also makes honey\*!

\* SO BE CAREFUL NOT TO KNOCK THE LEVER FROM MONEY TO HONEY WHEN YOU'RE MAKING MONEY. (THIS MEANS YOU, TERRY!)

## 94 Never-ending staircase

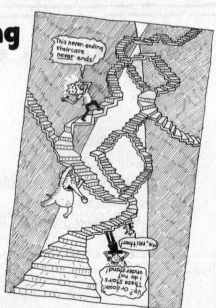

The truly amazing thing about our never-ending staircase is that, not only does it never end, it never actually starts either!

## 95 Two-Dollar Shop

There's nothing over two dollars in Pinchy McPhee's Two-Dollar Shop—bargains galore!

## 96 Two-Million-Dollar Shop

There's nothing under two million dollars in Fancy Fish's Two-Million-Dollar Shop—non-bargains galore!

# Refrigerator-throwing range

Fully equipped with all your refrigerator-throwing needs, including a refrigerator-vending machine, so the only reason you have to stop throwing refrigerators is either because you're too tired to throw any more or because you've been hit by too many refrigerators.

# Bunfighting level

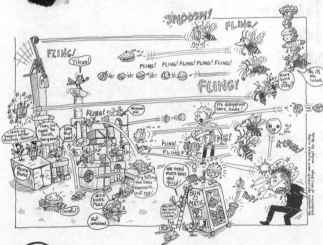

Fully equipped with all your bunfighting needs, including a bun-vending machine, so the only reason you have to stop throwing buns is either because you're too tired to throw any more or because you've been hit by too many buns.

WHAT'S WHERE

## 99 Mount Everest

At 8,849 metres, Mount Everest is the highest mountain in the world. Many people think it's located in the Himalayas but it's actually in our treehouse*.

* PLEASE DON'T TELL THE TIBETANS.

## 100 Burp bank

You never know when a burp might come in handy, so don't just burp them away into the atmosphere—put them in the bank!

# 101 Tangled-up level

Everything is really, really tangled up in our tangled-up level. And if you're silly— or careless— enough to enter, you will be too!

# 102 Deep-thoughts thinking room

Do you think deep thoughts or do deep thoughts think you? (Just one of the many deep thoughts you might have in our deep-thoughts thinking room!)

# 103 Mighty fortress

Our mighty fortress is reinforced with extra-strong fortress reinforcer, so don't even think about laying siege to it as you're sure to be disappointed.

# 104 Beautiful sunny meadow

Relax and/or frolic without a care in our beautiful sunny meadow full of buttercups, butterflies and bluebirds.

# Tiny-horse level

The problem with regular horses is that they're as big as regular horses, but our tiny-horse level has horses so tiny you can hold them in the palm of your hand!

# Pyjama-party room

Our pyjama-party room has everything you need for the ultimate pyjama party, including multi-bunk beds, a pyjama-vending machine and, best of all, no clocks so you never have to go to sleep!

# 107 Underpants Museum

Our Underpants Museum is home to the most complete collection of underpants—past, present and exploding—in the world.

# 108 Photo-bombing booth

Do you enjoy spoiling other people's photos by jumping into the background? You do? Well then, you are going to love the convenience of our photo-bombing booth!

## 109 Waiting room

Why are we waiting?
Because we're in the waiting
room, of course. (Duh!)

## 110 Treehouse visitor centre

Our visitor centre
has everything you
need to make the
most of your visit:
a 24-hour information
desk, a penguin-
powered flying
treehouse tour bus
and a gift shop.

WHAT'S WHERE

## 111 Door of Doom

Do not open our Door
of Doom under any
circumstances or you
will be completely and
utterly doomed*!

\* YOU HAVE BEEN WARNED.

## 112 Circus

Our circus is the greatest
show on Earth. It has fire-eaters,
sword-swallowers, chair-tamers,
trapeze artists and clowns!
Roll up! Roll up!

# All-you-can-eat-including-the-furniture level

Everything on this level is edible: the floor, the furniture and even you ... so dig in, eat up and watch out*!

\* IN CASE SOMEBODY TRIES TO EAT YOU!

# Kite-flying hill

The only thing better than flying a kite is being a kite that's being flown!

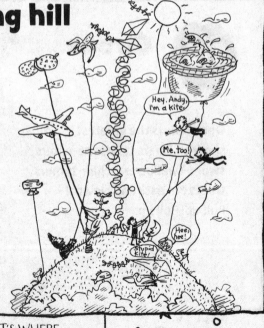

WHAT'S WHERE

# 115 Traffic school

Learn the rules of the road—or not—in our fun and educational traffic school.

# 116 Giant-fighting-robot arena

Fight like a robot in a giant-fighting-robot suit in our giant-fighting-robot arena. (Just watch out for Jill's right hook—it's a knockout!)

# Water-ski park

Water-ski parks are fun, but they're even more fun if the water is full of flesh-eating piranhas. Don't fall in!

# Soap bubble blaster

If you have to be caught in a blizzard, then make it a soap-bubble blizzard—it's the best sort of blizzard there is.

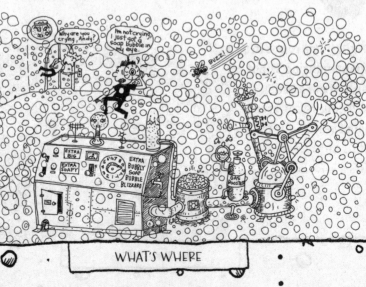

WHAT'S WHERE

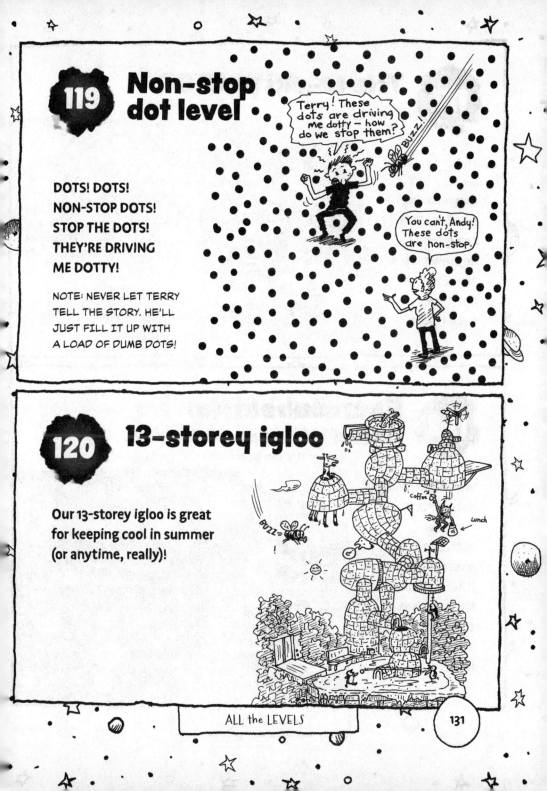

# The GRABINATOR

Our amazing GRABINATOR can grab anything from anywhere at any time, even itself!

# Extraterrestrial observation centre

We love observing extraterrestrials from our extraterrestrial observation centre (that is, when there are not too many planets and space junk in the way).

WHAT'S WHERE

## 123 Time-wasting level

When you've got some time to waste, our time-wasting level can help you waste it in the most time-efficient way possible.

## 124 Toilet paper factory

Why? Because you can never have too much toilet paper*!

* UNLESS YOU'RE IN A TOILET PAPER PLAGUE, OF COURSE.

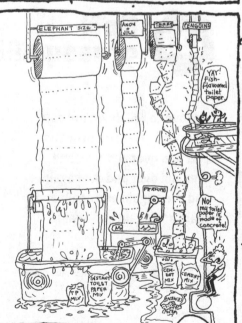

# 125 Giant juggling octopus

Juggling—and life—is eight times the fun with an eight-armed juggling octopus!

# 126 Soft grassy hill

We love to roll down our soft grassy hill over and over and over and over and over and over and over and over again. And then again and again and again and again and again.

NOTE: NO STEAMROLLERS ALLOWED! (THIS MEANS YOU, TERRY!)

## 127 Super long legs level

Some people look at super long legs and say 'Why?', but we look at super long legs and say 'Why not?!'

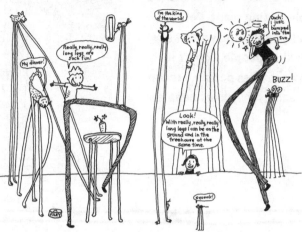

## 128 Treehouse fire brigade

Got a fire? Don't panic. Call the TFB* and they'll be there ASAP** TPTFO***.

\* TREEHOUSE FIRE BRIGADE.
\*\* AS SOON AS POSSIBLE.
\*\*\* TO PUT THE FIRE OUT.

##  129 People-eating plant

Our people-eating plant, Petal, really likes people, and when I say she really likes people, I don't just mean that she likes people, I mean that she really, *really* likes people.

## 130 Bookshop

Our bookshop-in-a-treehouse-in-a-tree-in-a-forest-in-a-book is the biggest—and best—bookshop-in-a-treehouse-in-a-tree-in-a-forest-in-a-book in the whole wide world!

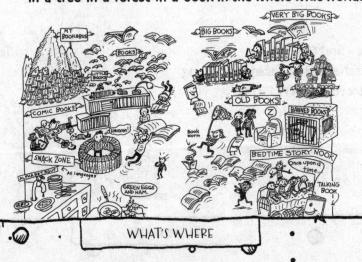

WHAT'S WHERE

# Word-o-matic

**131**

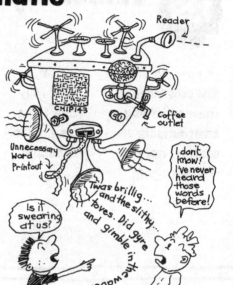

The word-o-matic knows every single word in the whole world*— even completely made-up ones and words that haven't even been made up yet!

*EXCEPT FOR QUAZJEX, WHICH IS TERRY'S CHEAT WORD IN SCRABBLE AND THE NAME OF HIS PET STUNT AXOLOTL.

# Recycling depot

**132**

In our recycling depot everything can be re-used, recycled, upcycled, downcycled or sideways-cycled into something else!

##  **Wrecking ball**

The only thing more satisfying than building stuff is knocking it down again!

##  **Camping ground**

Our camping ground has a lake, a playground, a campfire and a dark, dark wood*. And best of all, it's only a short drive from our kitchen in our all-terrain treehouse truck.

\* WHICH IS FULL OF HOBYAHS, SO WATCH OUT!

WHAT'S WHERE

# 135 Too-hard basket

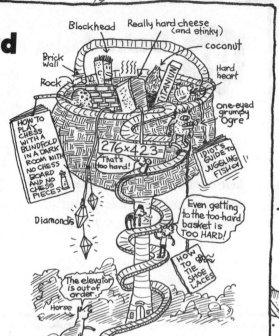

The too-hard basket contains all the stuff that's either too hard for us to eat, too hard for us to do or too hard for us to even think about.

# 136 SUPER BIG STUFF storey

Our SUPER BIG STUFF storey is where we keep all our super big stuff that's too super big to fit anywhere else.

# 137 Baked bean geyser

Love baked beans? Then you'll love our baked bean geyser—it erupts on the hour, every hour! (Don't love baked beans? Then avoid this level, especially on the hour, every hour.)

# 138 Ye Olde Worlde Historical Village

Travel back to a time when everything old and dumb was new and cool and had an 'e' on the end!

WHAT'S WHERE

## 139 — Fish milkshake bar

Love fish milkshakes? Then you must be either a penguin, a shark or a cat, and—unlike Terry, Jill and me—you will love the fish milkshake bar*!

\* FISH MILKSHAKES SERVED FRESH EVERY DAY BY OUR FISH MILKSHAKE SHARK BARTENDER.

## 140 — Complaining room

Love complaining? Then you'll love our complaining room. Hate complaining? Then come to the complaining room and complain about it.

## 141 Spooky graveyard

It's always midnight in the spooky graveyard, even in the middle of the day. *Whooo-oooo-ooooo-oooooo!*\*

\* GHOULISH GHOST AND SPOOKY
SKELETON SIGHTINGS GUARANTEED!

## 142 Toffee-apple orchard

The toffee-apple orchard is guarded by a kind scarecrow who likes children. As a result, there are not many toffee apples in the toffee-apple orchard.

## 143 Deep, dark cave with a real live fire-breathing dragon

Okay, we haven't actually ever seen the dragon, but we're pretty sure it's there because, as everybody knows, where there's smoke coming out of a deep, dark cave, there's sure to be a real live fire-breathing dragon inside.

## 144 Bouldering alley

The bouldering alley is just like a bowling alley except with boulders instead of bowling balls ... and you instead of bowling pins.

NOTE: PLEASE DON'T BOWL MORE THAN ONE BOULDER AT A TIME—ESPECIALLY IF IT'S MY TURN TO BE THE BOWLING PIN.

## 145 Wishing well

Terry has always wished for
a wishing well and now his wish
has come true.

## 146 Aquarium wonderland

Home to a bunch of
amazing aquatic
creatures, as well
as being the official
training centre for
Quazjex, the world's
greatest—and only—
stunt axolotl.

WHAT'S WHERE

# 147 Old boot camp

We built this level for the old boot we caught while fishing on the lake at our camping ground. Since then, it has become a home for old boots from all around the world.

# 148 Enigma engine

We're not exactly sure what the enigma engine does—that's why we called it the enigma* engine.

\* A RIDDLE WRAPPED INSIDE A MYSTERY INSIDE A PUZZLE.

## 149 World record breaking level

We've broken so many records on the world record breaking level that it's now a world record breaking world record breaking level!

## 150 Amazing mind-reading sandwich-making machine

If you can't decide what sort of sandwich you want, don't worry—the amazing sandwich-making machine will read your mind and make the sandwich that's exactly right for you.

WHAT'S WHERE

# TV quiz show level

Every treehouse needs a TV quiz show level, and who better to host it than Quizzy the quizzical quizbot—the quizzingest TV quiz show quizbot in the world!

NOTE: DON'T FORGET—QUIZZY WILL BE HOSTING A QUIZ AT THE END OF THIS BOOK. I HOPE YOU'VE BEEN PAYING ATTENTION!

# Lost property office

Whatever you've lost, you're sure to find it here in the lost property office—unless it's a sausage, of course, in which case you'll need to go to the lost sausage office (on level 153).

## 153 Lost sausage office

If it's a sausage you've lost, you're sure to find it here in the lost sausage office—unless it's not a sausage, of course, in which case you'll need to go to the lost property office (on level 152).

## 154 Spoontopia

Everybody knows that spoons are the friendliest types of cutlery there are—that's why we built Spoontopia, the spooniest and most spoontastic place on Earth!

# Super-stinky stuff level

**155**

BLOCK YOUR NOSE!
DON'T BREATHE!
DON'T EVER COME
IN HERE—AND IF
YOU'RE ALREADY
IN HERE GET OUT
FAST—WHILE YOU
STILL CAN!!!

# Billions of Birds™ level

**156**

To be honest, there's probably
not actually a billion birds here
but they make so much noise
(and mess) that there may
as well be.

# Santa Land

**157**

Santa Land is the land where we put all the Santa clones that were created when Santa fell into the cloning machine (on level 56). In Santa Land it's Christmas all year round!

# Potato-powered translation transmitter

**158**

Our potato-powered translation transmitter allows us to talk to anyone and any thing at any time. It can translate any language into any other language, and best of all, it's powered by potatoes so you can talk for as long as you like!

## 159 Electric pony stable

Our electric pony stable features everything an electric pony could wish for, including a fast-charging station and automatic hoof polishers!

## 160 Noisy level

The noisy level is the noisiest place in the treehouse, noisier even than the screeching balloon orchestra and the Billions of Birds™ levels put together! (Earplugs recommended.)

## 161 Monster level

Monsters are cool—everybody knows that—but creating a level full of them was pretty much the worst idea we've ever had. (We've only ever been in there once and we're too scared to ever go again!)

## 162 Hall of funhouse mirrors

You can be any size, shape or colour you want in our hall of funhouse mirrors. (You can even be upside down and inside out, though we don't recommend this.)

WHAT'S WHERE

# Kangaroo-riding range

**163**

If you like high-speed bouncing, then kangaroo-riding is for you. Our kangaroo-riding range offers plenty of space for you and your roo to bounce as high, as fast and for as long as you want.

---

# WHATEVER-WEATHER-YOU-WANT dome

**164**

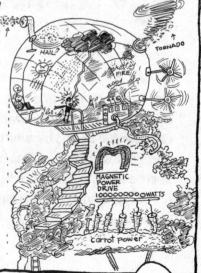

You can have whatever weather you want in our weather dome, whatever the weather outside!

NOTE: DON'T FORGET TO SHUT THE DOOR BEFORE STARTING UP THE WEATHER. (THIS MEANS YOU, TERRY!)

## 165 Gingerbread house

You can eat any part of the gingerbread house*, and the little old lady** who lives in it doesn't mind at all!

\* IF YOU'RE SEARCHING FOR THE GINGERBREAD HOUSE, DON'T BOTHER BECAUSE THE MIRROR GANG ATE IT ALL.
\*\* DITTO FOR THE LITTLE OLD LADY. THEY ATE HER TOO!

## 166 Gecko chamber

I really wanted an *echo* chamber, but Terry thought I said *gecko* chamber, so we ended up with a chamber full of geckos, which is fine; geckos are fun—not as fun as echoes, of course but, hey, it's better than a chamber full of nothing.

WHAT'S WHERE

# Paper plane research and development facility

Our paper planes are built to the highest possible specifications allowable for paper planes, with precision folding, aerodynamically enhanced paper, weighted nose cones and tiny, fully qualified paper pilots to ensure the safest and straightest-flying paper planes in the world.

# Treehouse in a treehouse

Sure, it's cool having a 169-storey treehouse but sometimes it's nice to get away from it all and chill out somewhere a little more cosy.

# Jill's house

We'd been wondering what to do with the 169th level and then, after Jill's house was blown away (Terry's fault!), we knew exactly what to do. We built her a new house right here so that she and all her animals could come and live in the treehouse with us. Yay!

Maaa!

Baaad!

WHAT'S WHERE

# PART THREE
# WHERE ELSE
## OTHER PLACES

If you're like most of our readers, you're probably wondering whether we spend all of our time in the treehouse. Well, no, actually. Sometimes we travel to other places—past, present and future. Here are a few of our favourite—and least favourite—places.

Tear in the fabric of the Universe

Koala noise!

Argh!

BEWARE OF CROCS

Ouch!

Grrr!

Goose

mallet.

# ANCIENT EGYPT
## (650 BC)

**Pharaohs! Pyramids! Mummies! What's not to like?**

(SEE *THE 65-STOREY TREEHOUSE*)

WHERE ELSE

# ANCIENT ROME
## (65 BC)

Chariot racing was the Ancient Romans' idea of fun, unless, of course, you were an Ancient Roman horse or chariot racer.

(SEE *THE 65-STOREY TREEHOUSE*)

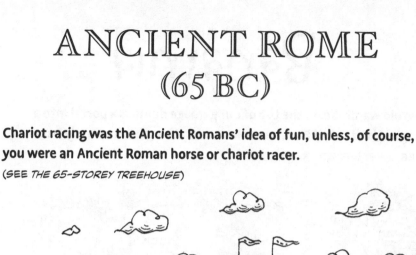

Please note that no horse drawings were injured in the making of this chapter.

# Banarnia

The old wardrobe on the top of our garbage dump is a portal into a
magical land called Banarnia (where everything is completely bananas).

(SEE *THE 91-STOREY TREEHOUSE*)

A big
duck

WHERE ELSE

# BIG NOSE BOOKS

The company that publishes our books, Big Nose Books,
is in a tall building in the city on the other side of the forest.

HERE WE SEE OUR PUBLISHER, MR BIG NOSE, IN HIS OFFICE JUST AS
*THE 39-STOREY TREEHOUSE* IS BEING DELIVERED
(RIGHT ON TIME, JUST LIKE ALL OUR BOOKS).

OTHER PLACES

# Blobdromeda

If you like mud, then Blobdromeda—made entirely of mud—is the planet for you! Populated by a race of peaceful, mud-dwelling blobs. Occasionally threatened by mud-sucking bog toads.

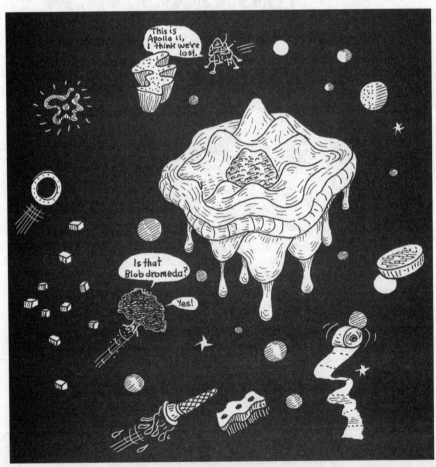

(SEE *THE 130-STOREY TREEHOUSE*)

WHERE ELSE

# Cheeseland

A theme park dedicated entirely to thrilling, cheese-based rides and attractions, including the infamous molten cheese whirlpool.

(SEE *THE 39-STOREY TREEHOUSE*)

# crabocene-era earth
## (650 million AD)

A horrible place ruled
by giant crabs.
**DO NOT GO THERE\*!**

\* UNLESS YOUR TIME
MACHINE MALFUNCTIONS
AND YOU END UP THERE
BY ACCIDENT.
(SEE *THE 65-STOREY TREEHOUSE*)

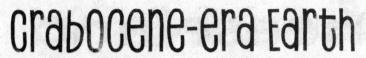

# DARK SIDE OF THE MOON

The dark side of the moon is much darker than the other side
of the moon. Once home to Professor Stupido (the world's
greatest un-inventor) during his exile from Earth.
(SEE *THE 39-STOREY TREEHOUSE*)

THE DARK SIDE
OF THE MOON
POPULATION: 1

WHERE ELSE

# EYEBALLIA

A planet full of giant flying eyeballs who host an annual intergalactic death battle.

(SEE *THE 130-STOREY TREEHOUSE*)

*Fairyland*

The place where all the fairies live . . . also where the tooth fairy takes all the teeth she collects.

(SEE *THE 104-STOREY TREEHOUSE*)

OTHER PLACES

# Filing Island

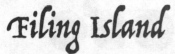

The most well-organised island on Earth where all the plants and animals are filed alphabetically in filing cabinets.

(SEE *THE 117-STOREY TREEHOUSE*)

# FOREST

Our treehouse is situated in a large forest and on the other side of the forest is our friend Jill's house.

# future eqrtH
## (65,000 Ad)

A totally danger-proof world in which it is impossible to hurt—or be hurt by—anything or anybody.

(SEE *THE 65-STOREY TREEHOUSE*)

# GIANT GORILLA'S ISLAND

A far, far, far away island, home to a giant gorilla that loves giant bananas.

BEWARE GIANT APE

(SEE *THE 13-STOREY TREEHOUSE*)

# JILL'S ANIMAL EARLY LEARNING CENTRE

**An early learning centre ... for animals only\*!**

\* AND ME AND TERRY AFTER OUR MINDS
WERE EMPTIED IN BANARNIA.
(SEE *THE 91-STOREY TREEHOUSE*)

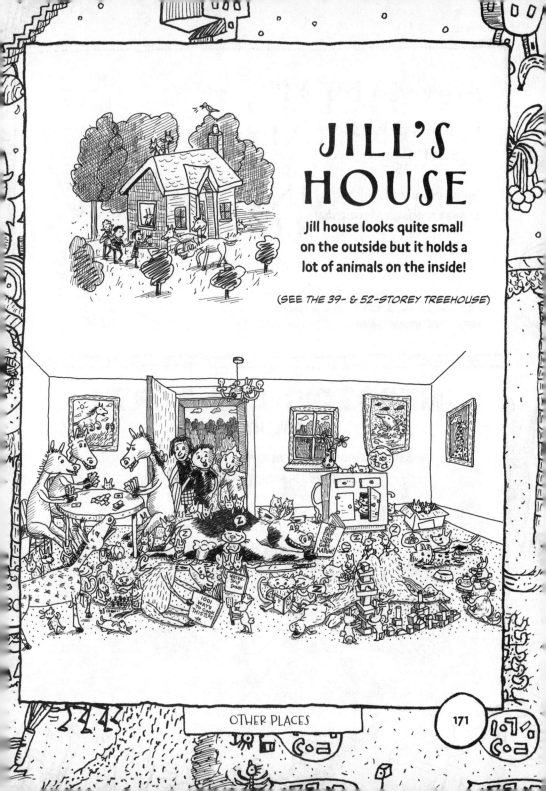

# JILL'S HOUSE

Jill house looks quite small on the outside but it holds a lot of animals on the inside!

(SEE *THE 39- & 52-STOREY TREEHOUSE*)

# Mermaidia's undersea castle

**Home of our enemy, the sea monster Mermaidia!**

NOTE: AND DON'T BE FOOLED BY THE PROMISE OF FREE AIR . . . IT'S A TRICK. (SEE *TREEHOUSE TALES*)

# MESOZOIC-ERA EARTH
## (65 MILLION BC)

**Dinosaurs, dinosaurs, dinosaurs . . . and more dinosaurs!**

(SEE *THE 65-STOREY TREEHOUSE*)

WHERE ELSE

# Monkey house

Before Terry and I wrote books we used to work at the zoo in the monkey house—cleaning it out and filling in for the monkeys when they were on their breaks.

(SEE *THE 13- & 169-STOREY TREEHOUSE*)

# Pre-Cambrian-era Earth (650 million BC)

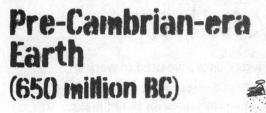

Quite hot and home to a puddle full of prehistoric pond scum, some of the earliest life forms on Earth.

(SEE *THE 65-STOREY TREEHOUSE*)

# Stone-age Earth (65,000 BC)

Stone, stone, stone . . . and more stone! If you like stone, then you'll love Stone-age Earth!

(SEE *THE 65-STOREY TREEHOUSE*)

# THE 13-STOREY TREEHOUSE SCHOOL

Formerly known as Gradgrind Academy*,
The 13-Storey Treehouse School is a
state-of-the-art educational facility
built by us with the help of the school
principal, teachers, students and
the mirror gang.

In addition to a range of innovative
classrooms and an inflatable library, it
also features a high-speed water slide,
a deep hole and an ice-cream factory.

\* DESTROYED BY MONKEYS.

(SEE *THE 169-STOREY TREEHOUSE*)

9 THEATRE (Drama)

16 LOW WATER SLIDE

2 UNDERGROUND LABORATOR
(chemistry)

THE 13-STOREY
TREEHOUSE
SCHOOL

202

1 ICE-CREAM FACTORY
(canteen)

WHERE ELSE

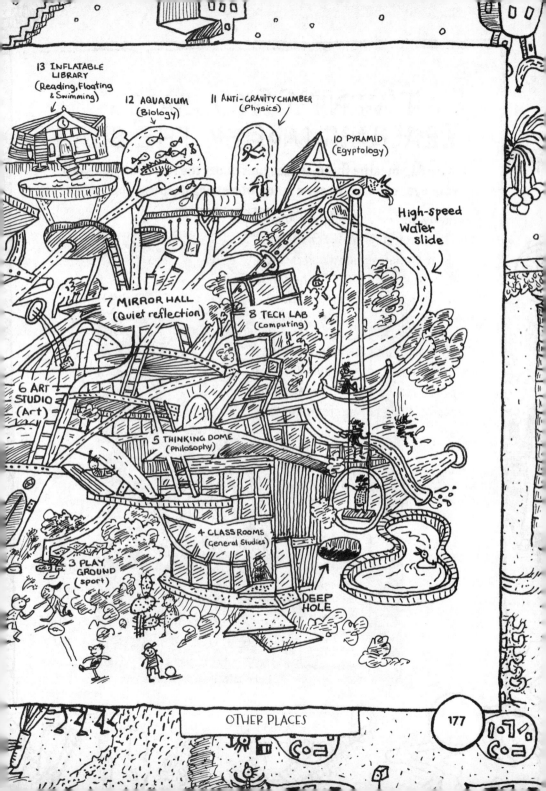

13 INFLATABLE LIBRARY (Reading, Floating & Swimming)

12 AQUARIUM (Biology)

11 ANTI-GRAVITY CHAMBER (Physics)

10 PYRAMID (Egyptology)

High-speed Water slide

7 MIRROR HALL (Quiet reflection)

8 TECH LAB (Computing)

6 ART STUDIO (Art)

5 THINKING DOME (Philosophy)

4 CLASS ROOMS (General Studies)

3 PLAY GROUND (sport)

DEEP HOLE

# TWENTY THOUSAND LEAGUES UNDER THE SEA

It's hard to breathe this many leagues under the sea, but if you keep your eyes open, you'll see a lot of interesting deep-sea creatures.

(SEE *THE 91-STOREY TREEHOUSE*)

SINK
-O-
METER™

1000 LEAGUES
2000 LEAGUES
3000 LEAGUES
4000 LEAGUES
5000 LEAGUES
6000 LEAGUES
7000 LEAGUES
8000 LEAGUES
9000 LEAGUES
10000 LEAGUES
11000 LEAGUES
12000 LEAGUES
13000 LEAGUES
14000 LEAGUES
15000 LEAGUES
16000 LEAGUES
17000 LEAGUES
18000 LEAGUES
19000 LEAGUES
20000 LEAGUES

WHERE ELSE

# VEGETABLE KINGDOM

Vegetables, vegetables, vegetables . . .
and more vegetables!
If you love vegetables, you'll love
the Vegetable Kingdom!
(SEE *THE 52-STOREY TREEHOUSE*)

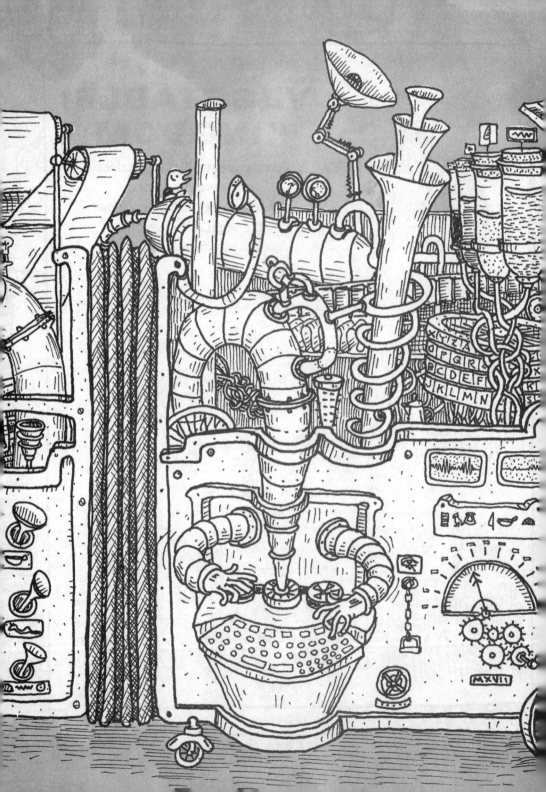

# PART FOUR
# WHAT ELSE
## ALL the GADGETS and GIZMOS

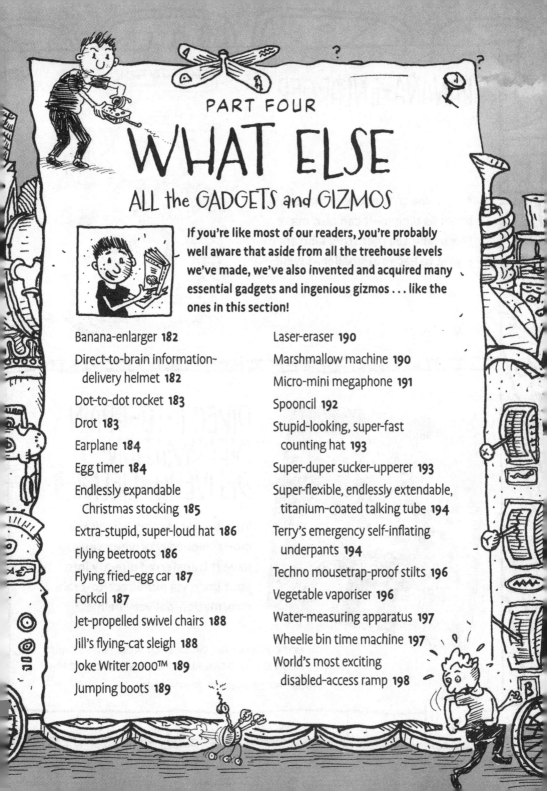

If you're like most of our readers, you're probably well aware that aside from all the treehouse levels we've made, we've also invented and acquired many essential gadgets and ingenious gizmos ... like the ones in this section!

# BANANA-ENLARGER

A machine that not only makes bananas bigger—it can also make them (and sea monsters who are trying to eat you) smaller as well!

(SEE *THE 13-STOREY TREEHOUSE*)

# DIRECT-TO-BRAIN INFORMATION-DELIVERY HELMET

Why bother reading a book the old-fashioned way when you can have it transferred directly into your brain via our direct-to-brain information-delivery helmet?

NOTE: HASN'T ACTUALLY BEEN INVENTED YET AND, WHEN IT HAS BEEN, MAY CAUSE INJURY OR DEATH.

(SEE *THE 13-STOREY TREEHOUSE*)

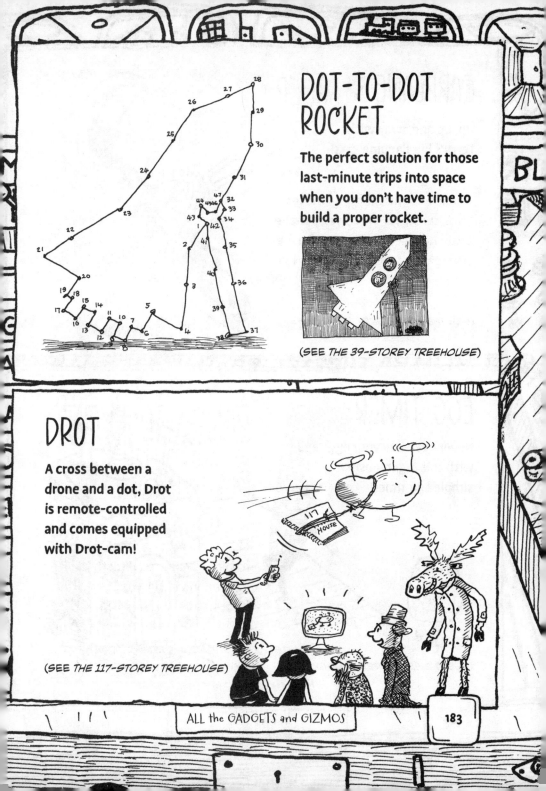

# DOT-TO-DOT ROCKET

The perfect solution for those last-minute trips into space when you don't have time to build a proper rocket.

(SEE *THE 39-STOREY TREEHOUSE*)

# DROT

A cross between a drone and a dot, Drot is remote-controlled and comes equipped with Drot-cam!

(SEE *THE 117-STOREY TREEHOUSE*)

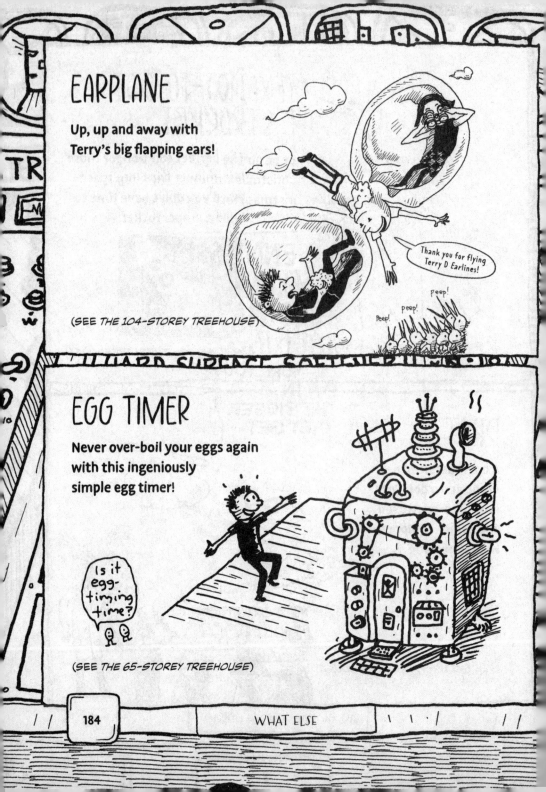

# EARPLANE

Up, up and away with
Terry's big flapping ears!

Thank you for flying
Terry D Earlines!

peep!

peep!

peep.

(SEE *THE 104-STOREY TREEHOUSE*)

# EGG TIMER

Never over-boil your eggs again
with this ingeniously
simple egg timer!

Is it
egg-
timing
time?

(SEE *THE 65-STOREY TREEHOUSE*)

# ENDLESSLY EXPANDABLE CHRISTMAS STOCKINGS

**Worried that Santa might not be able to fit all the presents on your Santa list into your Christmas stocking? Never fear! Endlessly expandable Christmas stockings are here!**

NEW ENDLESSLY EXPANDABLE* CHRISTMAS STOCKINGS

THE MORE YOU PUT IN.... THE BIGGER THEY GET

* GUARANTEED TO EXPAND MORE THAN 500 TIMES ORIGINAL SIZE WITHOUT EXPLODING!

(SEE *THE 156-STOREY TREEHOUSE*)

# EXTRA-STUPID, SUPER-LOUD HAT

Extra-stupid, super-loud hats
can be super loud and a lot of fun,
but they're quite annoying if
you are trying to sleep.

(SEE *THE 104-STOREY TREEHOUSE*)

# FLYING BEETROOTS

The only truly reliable
and safe vegetable-based
form of air travel.

(SEE *THE 39-STOREY TREEHOUSE*)

# FLYING FRIED-EGG CAR

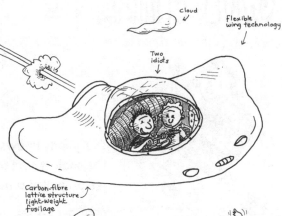

cloud

flexible wing technology

Two idiots

You can fly or drive around completely unnoticed in this flying car cunningly disguised as a fried egg.

Carbon-fibre lattice structure light-weight fusilage

Bird →

(SEE *THE 52-STOREY TREEHOUSE*)

## FORKCIL

NEW **FORKCIL**
UNBELIEVABLE
IT'S A **FORK**
AND A **PENCIL**
AT THE **SAME TIME!**

Food

Forkcil

Jill

CHOMP CHOMP

Drawing

Drawing

You can DRAW and EAT at the SAME time with FORKCIL!

(IT REALLY WORKS)

Jill's take on Terry's classic design for the spooncil. It allows you to draw and fork food into your mouth at the same time!

(SEE *THE 169-STOREY TREEHOUSE*)

# JET-PROPELLED SWIVEL CHAIRS

Everybody knows that swivel chairs are the coolest sort of chairs there are. Well, jet-propelled swivel chairs are even cooler.

(SEE *THE 39- & 104-STOREY TREEHOUSE*)

# JILL'S FLYING-CAT SLEIGH

Thirteen flying cats plus one pram plus one Jill equals one Jill's flying-cat sleigh!

(SEE *THE 13-, 26- & 104-STOREY TREEHOUSE*)

WHAT ELSE

# JOKE WRITER 2000™

Whatever you're writing it will be 110% funnier if written by a Joke Writer 2000™—the pen that can write by itself*!

\* THIS WAS WRITTEN BY A JOKE WRITER 2000™.

(SEE *THE 104-STOREY TREEHOUSE*)

# JUMPING BOOTS

If you're taking part in a jumping contest, get the jump on your competition by wearing these amazing spring-loaded jumping boots.

(SEE *TREEHOUSE TALES*)

# LASER-ERASER

For those erasing
emergencies when a
regular eraser is just
not big—or fast—enough.

> I hereby erase
> Andy's badly drawn cat.
> Take that, mutant-lion thing,
> And that,
> And that,
> And THAT!

(SEE *THE 39-STOREY TREEHOUSE*)

# MARSHMALLOW MACHINE

Follows you around and
fires marshmallows into
your mouth whenever it
detects you are hungry.

(SEE *THE 13-, 39- & 143-STOREY TREEHOUSE*)

# MICRO-MINI MEGAPHONE

Do you find it difficult communicating with giants? Then try Terry's micro-mini megaphone. It amplifies tiny voices and is perfectly designed for even the tiniest of hands to hold.

(SEE *THE 65-STOREY TREEHOUSE*)

TERRY's NEW
MICRO-MINI
MEGAPHONE
(IT REALLY WORKS)

ANOTHER FABULOUS
TERRY INVENTION

TALKING
TO
GIANTS
HAS NEVER
BEEN SO
EASY!!

# SPOONCIL

**Would you like to be able to draw and eat
at the same time? Well, now you can!**

NOTE: SPOONCILS ARE ALSO USEFUL FOR DIGGING YOUR WAY
OUT OF STORYTELLING JAIL WHEN YOU'VE BEEN LOCKED UP BY
THE STORY POLICE FOR ONE BILLION YEARS.

(SEE *THE 39- & 117-STOREY TREEHOUSE*)

# STUPID-LOOKING, SUPER-FAST COUNTING HAT

**Ideal for when you need a lot of things counted and you need them counted fast and you don't mind looking stupid while counting them!**

(SEE *THE 104-STOREY TREEHOUSE*)

# SUPER-DUPER SUCKER-UPPERER

Ten times more powerful than a vacuum cleaner and twenty times stronger than an industrial exhaust fan: the super-duper sucker-upperer is guaranteed to help you clean up even the biggest mess in no time at all*.

\* IT WILL ALSO SUCK UP TIME. HANDLE WITH CARE.
(SEE *TREEHOUSE TALES*)

# SUPER-FLEXIBLE, ENDLESSLY EXTENDABLE,

## TERRY'S EMERGENCY SELF-INFLATING UNDERPANTS

FLOOF!

whoosh!

A pair of underpants that automatically inflate on contact with water in order to protect the wearer (i.e. Terry) from drowning. Can also be used for air travel.

Terry

emergency self-inflating underpants

(SEE THE 26-, 78-, 91- & 169-STOREY TREEHOUSE)

# TITANIUM-COATED TALKING TUBE

**Great way to communicate over long distances with people (like Jill) who don't have a phone.**

(SEE *THE 26-STOREY TREEHOUSE*)

# TECHNO MOUSETRAP-PROOF STILTS

(SEE *THE 78-STOREY TREEHOUSE*)

If you want to steal the chips in my high-tech potato chip storage facility, you're going to need a pair of these to evade the 1000 loaded mousetraps that surround my chip safe. Wait— why am I telling you this? Forget I said anything . . . and don't try to steal my chips!

# VEGETABLE VAPORISER

Vaporises any vegetables within 50 metres to ensure there's no danger of them getting into anyone's mouth and making them healthy.

NO!! A BRUSSEL SPROUT!!

VAPORISE!!

YAY!!

GRRR!!

(SEE *THE 13-STOREY TREEHOUSE*)

# WATER-MEASURING APPARATUS

Essential secret laboratory mechanism capable of adding as little as one drop of water at a time to sea-monkey eggs in order to avoid adding too much water.

(SEE *THE 13-STOREY TREEHOUSE*)

# WHEELIE BIN TIME MACHINE

The (im)perfect solution for those last-minute time travel trips into the past and/or future when you don't have time to build a proper time machine.

(SEE *THE 65-STOREY TREEHOUSE*)

interior of time machine

This is the outer wall of the bin. (Really!)

travelling through time

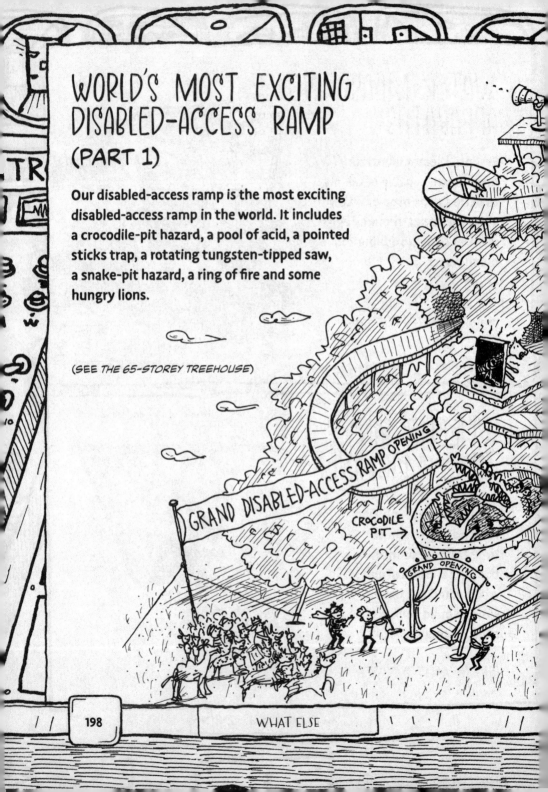

# WORLD'S MOST EXCITING DISABLED-ACCESS RAMP (PART 1)

Our disabled-access ramp is the most exciting disabled-access ramp in the world. It includes a crocodile-pit hazard, a pool of acid, a pointed sticks trap, a rotating tungsten-tipped saw, a snake-pit hazard, a ring of fire and some hungry lions.

(SEE *THE 65-STOREY TREEHOUSE*)

GRAND DISABLED-ACCESS RAMP OPENING

CROCODILE PIT →

GRAND OPENING

WHAT ELSE

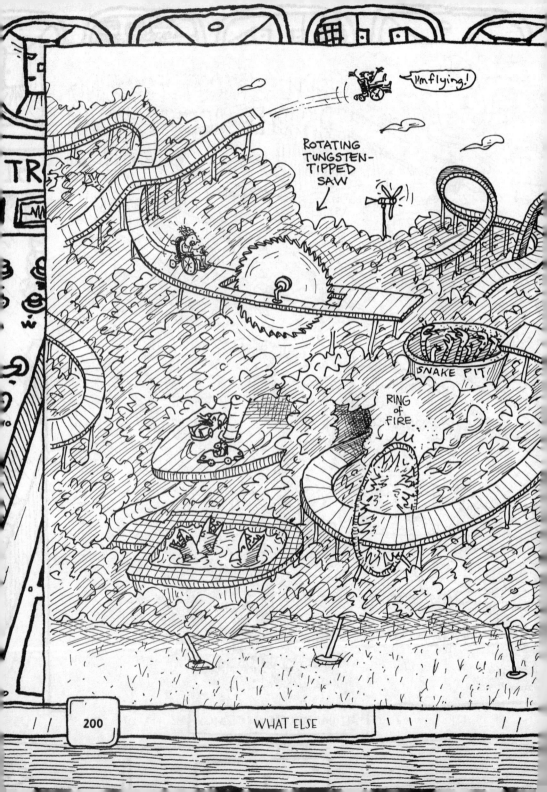

Hot chocolate ←

Cold chocolate

PART FIVE

# WHAT HAPPENS WHERE

## ALL the BOOKS

If you're like most of our readers, you probably want to know whether this guide contains a complete list of Treehouse books. Well, guess what? It does . . . and there's a little summary of each one as well.

NOTE: THIS IS THE ORDER THE BOOKS WERE PUBLISHED IN, BUT THEY CAN BE READ IN ANY ORDER.

The 13-Storey Treehouse

The 26-Storey Treehouse

The 39-Storey Treehouse

The 52-Storey Treehouse

The 65-Storey Treehouse

The 78-Storey Treehouse

The 91-Storey Treehouse

The 104-Storey Treehouse

The 117-Storey Treehouse

The 130-Storey Treehouse

The 143-Storey Treehouse

The 156-Storey Treehouse

The 169-Storey Treehouse

Treehouse Tales

The Treehouse Joke Book 1

The Treehouse Joke Book 2

The Treehouse Fun Books 1, 2, 3 & Bumper!

Really hot chocolate

I'm staying until after 9

mine don't fit.

I'm not!

It's my Mr. BigNose doll.

## The 13-STOREY TREEHOUSE

This is the one about a typical day in the treehouse, where we deal with flying cats, sea-monkeys, sea monsters, mermaids, real monkeys and a giant gorilla.

## The 26-STOREY TREEHOUSE

This is the one where I tell the story of how Terry, Jill and I all met, how the treehouse got built and why we hate pirates (especially Captain Woodenhead!).

WHAT HAPPENS WHERE

# The 39-STOREY TREEHOUSE

This is the one where Terry invents a machine to write and draw the book for us, but it goes out of control and we have to get the world's greatest un-inventor, Professor Stupido, to un-invent it . . . which is when the *real* trouble begins.

# The 52-STOREY TREEHOUSE

This is the one where our publisher, Mr Big Nose, has been kidnapped by angry vegetables and we have to go undercover, deep into the heart of the Vegetable Kingdom, to rescue him.

## The 65-STOREY TREEHOUSE

This is the one where we go time-travelling in our malfunctioning wheelie bin time machine in an attempt to get a building permit for the treehouse.

## The 78-STOREY TREEHOUSE

This is the one where Hollywood director Mr Big Shot comes to the treehouse to make *Treehouse: The Movie* but, thanks to a best-friend-stealing gibbon and a bunch of spy cows, things don't turn out quite the way we'd hoped.

# The 91-STOREY TREEHOUSE

This is the one where we have to babysit Mr Big Nose's grandchildren and make sure they don't come to any harm, which is not easy in our treehouse because even though it's a lot of fun, it's also the most dangerous treehouse in the world.

# The 104-STOREY TREEHOUSE

This is the one where I have the world's worst toothache and I'm in so much pain I can't write the book without the help of a Joke Writer 2000™. But getting one proves to be even more challenging than enduring the world's worst toothache.

# The 117-STOREY TREEHOUSE

This is the one where Terry takes over the narration and tells a really dumb story about dots, which is so dumb we end up having to go on the run from the Story Police who want to arrest us for crimes against storytelling. Along the way we meet famous children's writers Beatrix Potty, Boris Bendback and Dr Moose.

# The 130-STOREY TREEHOUSE

This is the one where we—and the treehouse *and* the tree—get abducted by a giant flying eyeball from Eyeballia and are forced to take part in an intergalactic death battle.

# The 143-STOREY TREEHOUSE

This is the one where we go camping on our camping ground level and end up having the scariest, most disastrous and un-relaxing camping holiday ever!

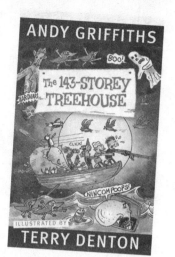

# The 156-STOREY TREEHOUSE

This is the one where our Christmas Eve preparations are interrupted by having to deal with an angry publisher, an evil snowman and dozens of cloned, over-excited Santas—all of whom threaten Christmas not only for us but for all the children of the world.

# The 169-STOREY TREEHOUSE

This is the one where we do battle with our WHATEVER-WEATHER-YOU-WANT dome, our doppelgangers (Anti-Andy, Terrible-Terry and Junkyard-Jill) and a truancy officer intent on capturing us and making us go to school.

# TREEHOUSE TALES:
## TOO SILLY TO BE TOLD . . . UNTIL NOW!

This is the one where I tell you 13 short treehouse stories that were too silly to be told . . . until now!

## WHO'S WHO and WHAT'S WHERE in the TREEHOUSE

This is the one you're holding in your hand right now! It's the greatest and most comprehensive guide to all the characters, levels, places, gadgets, gizmos and books in the Treehouse series you could wish for!

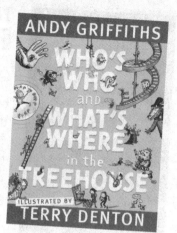

## The TREEHOUSE JOKE BOOK 1

If you're like most of our readers, you're probably wondering what our favourite jokes and riddles are. Well, they're all in here!

## The TREEHOUSE JOKE BOOK 2

If you're like most of our readers, you're probably wondering what jokes and riddles we left out of *The Treehouse Joke Book 1*. Well, here they are!

## The TREEHOUSE FUN BOOK

If you're like most of our readers, you're probably wondering what we do for fun when we're not writing books or having adventures—well, we do Treehouse Fun Books!

Stuff to write!
Pictures to draw!
Puzzles to solve!
And so much more!

## The TREEHOUSE FUN BOOK 2

More stuff to write!
More pictures to draw!
More puzzles to solve!
And much much more!

# The TREEHOUSE FUN BOOK 3

Even more stuff to write!
Even more pictures to draw!
Even more puzzles to solve!
And even much much more!

# THE BUMPER! TREEHOUSE FUN BOOK

This is the one that is packed with over 300 pages of Treehouse-inspired fun! (Contains the funnest activities from Treehouse Fun Books 1, 2 and 3 plus a whole heap of brand-new ones.)

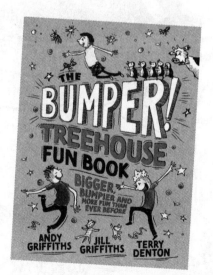

PART SIX

# WHO? WHAT? WHERE?
## The QUIZ

Greetings, Quizzlings! I am Quizzy the quizzical quizbot. You might remember meeting me on my TV quiz show (on level 151). You do? That's wonderful! Now let's see what else you remember and how much you know about the treehouse by taking this 30-question Treehouse quiz. Good luck—and no peeking at the answers on page 232 until you've finished!

*I'm outta here!*

*I haven't a clue!*

## Question 1
**If Mr Big Nose gets angry:**

○ a) his teeth drop out
○ b) his ears fall off
○ c) his nose gets bigger and bigger
○ d) he turns into a werewolf

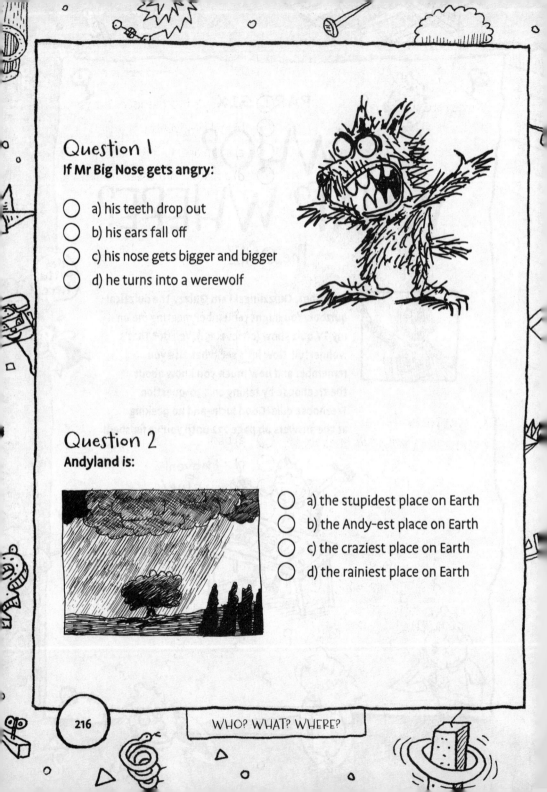

## Question 2
**Andyland is:**

○ a) the stupidest place on Earth
○ b) the Andy-est place on Earth
○ c) the craziest place on Earth
○ d) the rainiest place on Earth

WHO? WHAT? WHERE?

## Question 3
**Professor Stupido is:**

- a) Andy's nickname for Terry
- b) an UN-inventor
- c) a rap artist
- d) a history professor

Crazy!!

## Question 4
**Barky the Barking Dog likes to:**

- a) bark
- b) meow
- c) buzz
- d) moo

BARK!

Shh!

## Question 5
**Terry has a pair of emergency inflatable:**

- ○ a) scissors
- ○ b) underpants
- ○ c) friends
- ○ d) bananas

## Question 6
**What does the marshmallow machine shoot into your mouth?**

- ○ a) potatoes
- ○ b) ping pong balls
- ○ c) maggots
- ○ d) marshmallows

WHO? WHAT? WHERE?

## Question 7
**If you lost a sausage, you would look for it in:**

- ○ a) the lost property office
- ○ b) the sausage tank
- ○ c) the lost sausage office
- ○ d) Sausage Land

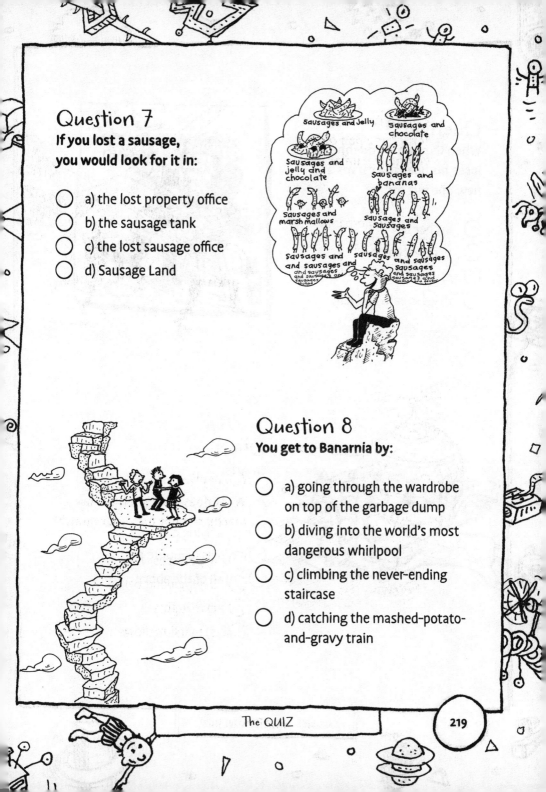

sausages and jelly

sausages and chocolate

sausages and jelly and chocolate

sausages and bananas

sausages and marsh mallows

sausages and sausages

sausages and sausages and sausages and sausages and sausages and sausages and sausages

sausages and sausages and sausages and sausages and sausages and sausages and sausages

## Question 8
**You get to Banarnia by:**

- ○ a) going through the wardrobe on top of the garbage dump
- ○ b) diving into the world's most dangerous whirlpool
- ○ c) climbing the never-ending staircase
- ○ d) catching the mashed-potato-and-gravy train

## Question 9

**When Captain Woodenhead loses his head, he carves a new one out of:**

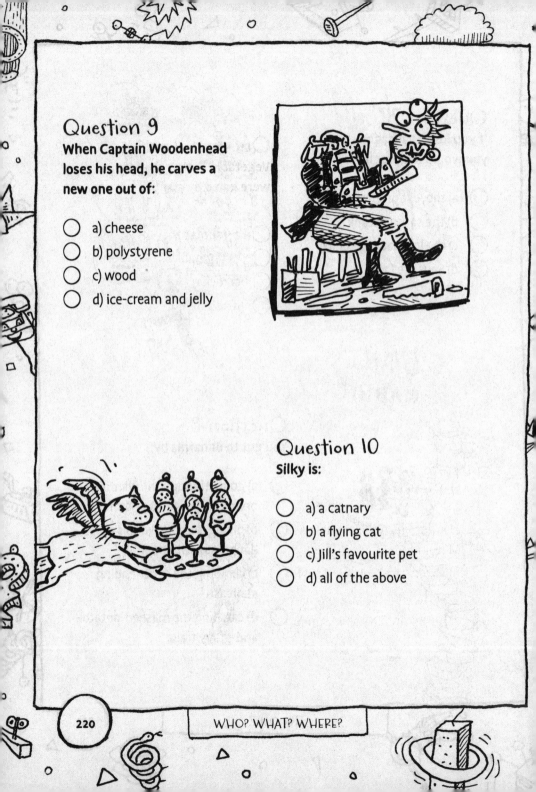

- ○ a) cheese
- ○ b) polystyrene
- ○ c) wood
- ○ d) ice-cream and jelly

## Question 10

**Silky is:**

- ○ a) a catnary
- ○ b) a flying cat
- ○ c) Jill's favourite pet
- ○ d) all of the above

WHO? WHAT? WHERE?

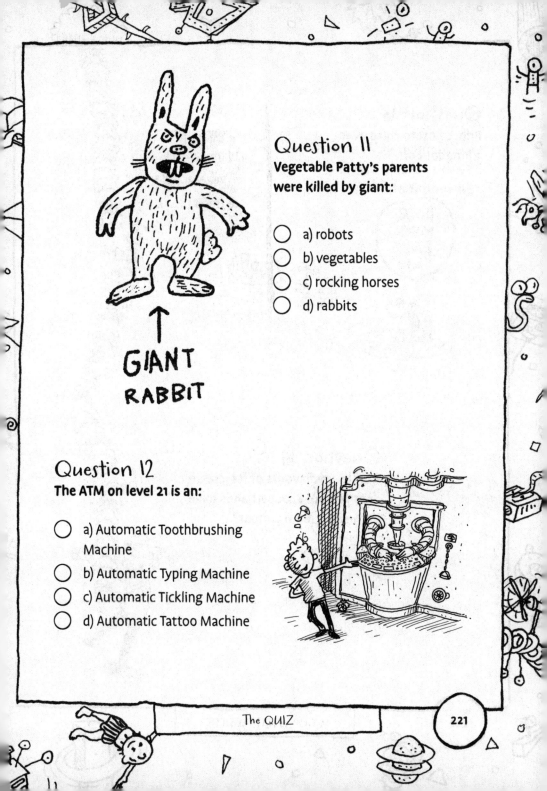

## Question 11
**Vegetable Patty's parents were killed by giant:**

○ a) robots
○ b) vegetables
○ c) rocking horses
○ d) rabbits

GIANT
RABBIT

## Question 12
**The ATM on level 21 is an:**

○ a) Automatic Toothbrushing Machine
○ b) Automatic Typing Machine
○ c) Automatic Tickling Machine
○ d) Automatic Tattoo Machine

## Question 13
**Prince Potato rules over a kingdom of:**

- ○ a) toy soldiers
- ○ b) pineapples
- ○ c) vegetables
- ○ d) frogs

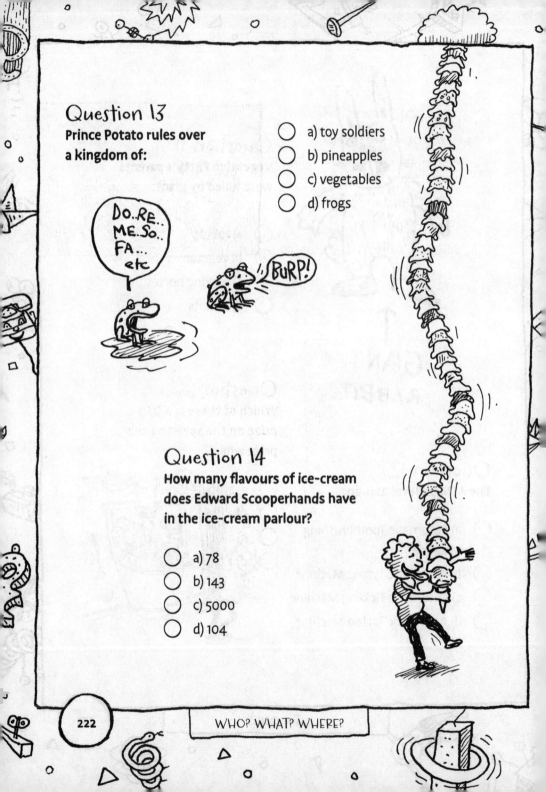

## Question 14
**How many flavours of ice-cream does Edward Scooperhands have in the ice-cream parlour?**

- ○ a) 78
- ○ b) 143
- ○ c) 5000
- ○ d) 104

WHO? WHAT? WHERE?

## Question 15
**Jill's three horses are called:**

- ○ a) Inky, Pinky and Ponky
- ○ b) Larry, Curly and Moe
- ○ c) Blarp, Pip and Pop
- ○ d) Flopsy, Mopsy and Cottontail

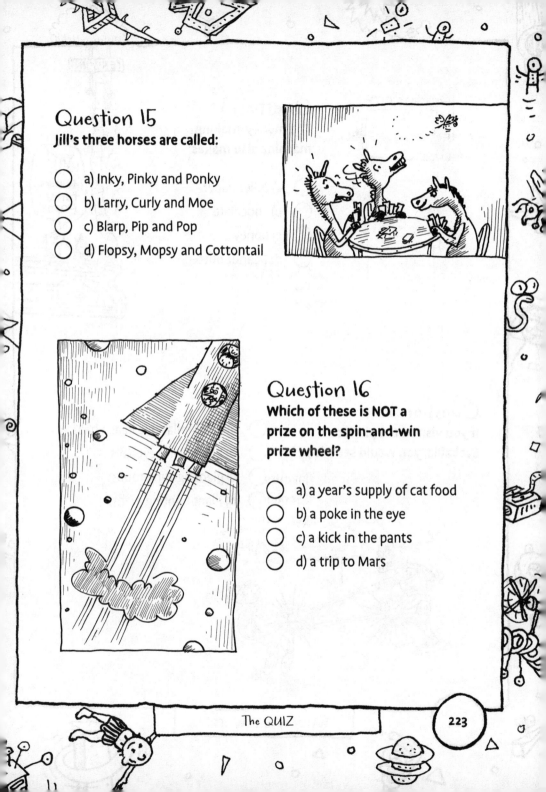

## Question 16
**Which of these is NOT a prize on the spin-and-win prize wheel?**

- ○ a) a year's supply of cat food
- ○ b) a poke in the eye
- ○ c) a kick in the pants
- ○ d) a trip to Mars

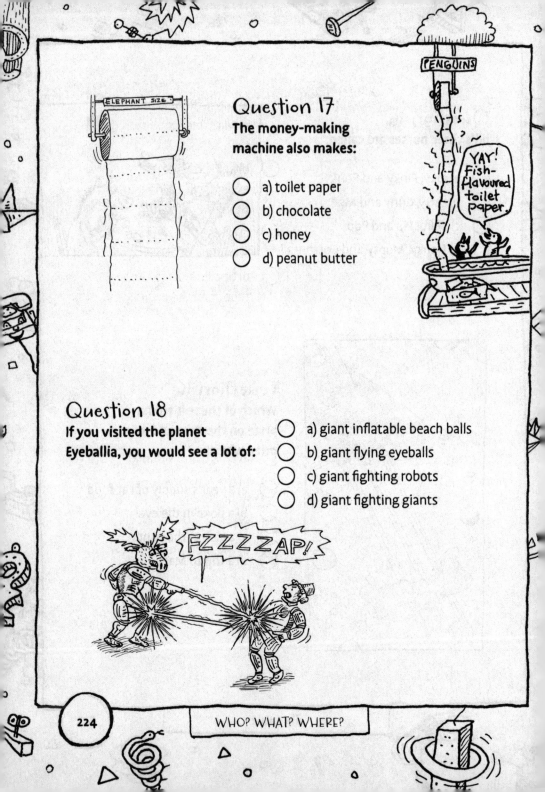

ELEPHANT SIZE

PENGUINS

YAY! Fish-flavoured toilet paper.

## Question 17
**The money-making machine also makes:**

○ a) toilet paper
○ b) chocolate
○ c) honey
○ d) peanut butter

## Question 18
**If you visited the planet Eyeballia, you would see a lot of:**

○ a) giant inflatable beach balls
○ b) giant flying eyeballs
○ c) giant fighting robots
○ d) giant fighting giants

FZZZZAP!

WHO? WHAT? WHERE?

## Question 19

**The official name of Terry's long-distance talking device is:**

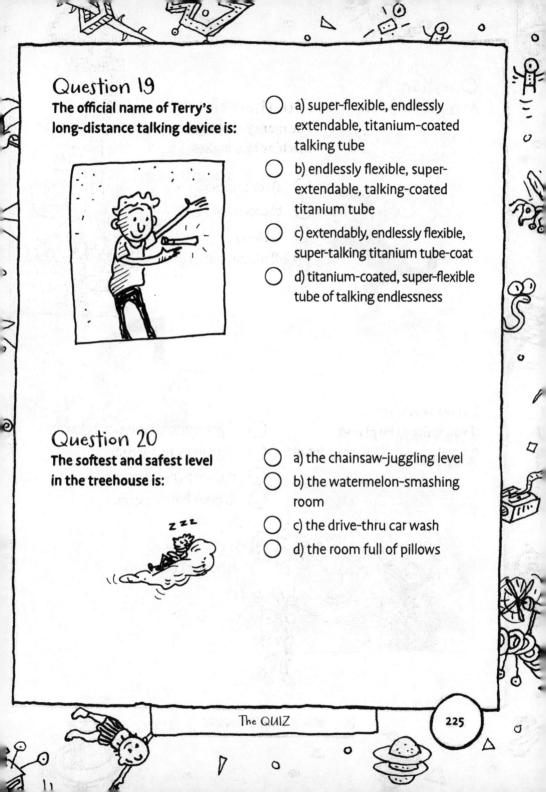

○ a) super-flexible, endlessly extendable, titanium-coated talking tube

○ b) endlessly flexible, super-extendable, talking-coated titanium tube

○ c) extendably, endlessly flexible, super-talking titanium tube-coat

○ d) titanium-coated, super-flexible tube of talking endlessness

## Question 20

**The softest and safest level in the treehouse is:**

z zz

○ a) the chainsaw-juggling level

○ b) the watermelon-smashing room

○ c) the drive-thru car wash

○ d) the room full of pillows

# Question 21
**Andy and Terry hate:**

- a) monkeys
- b) pirates
- c) vegetables
- d) all of the above

# Question 22
**Andy and Terry love:**

- a) monkeys
- b) pirates
- c) vegetables
- d) none of the above

WHO? WHAT? WHERE?

## Question 23
**Anti-Andy, Terrible-Terry and Junkyard-Jill are:**

○ a) Andy, Terry and Jill's doppelgangers

○ b) evil puppets

○ c) flavours of ice-cream

○ d) members of Captain Woodenhead's pirate crew

WATERMELON WHAMMY

GOLDFISH SURPRISE

FLYING MONKEY

## Question 24
**The treehouse disabled-access ramp is:**

○ a) the safest one in the world

○ b) the shortest one in the world

○ c) the most boring one in the world

○ d) the most exciting one in the world

## Question 25
**Everything on the Filing Island has been filed:**

○ a) numerically
○ b) alphabetically
○ c) by colour
○ d) by size from smallest to largest

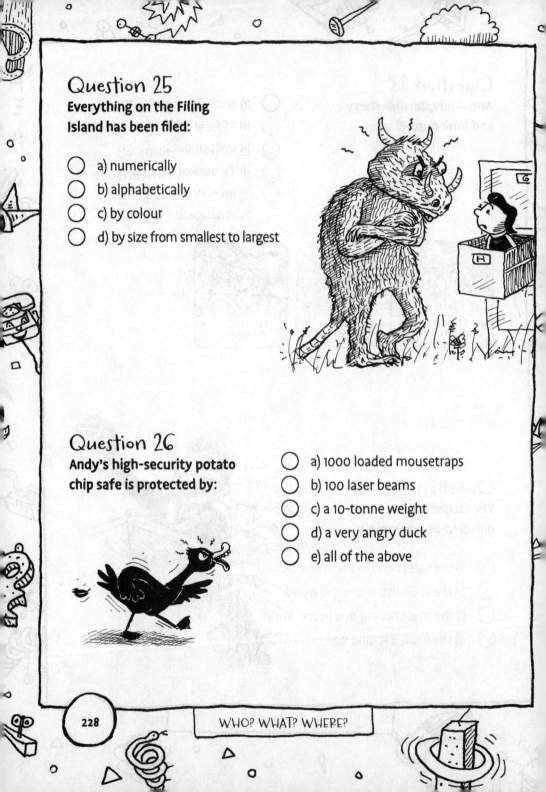

## Question 26
**Andy's high-security potato chip safe is protected by:**

○ a) 1000 loaded mousetraps
○ b) 100 laser beams
○ c) a 10-tonne weight
○ d) a very angry duck
○ e) all of the above

WHO? WHAT? WHERE?

## Question 27

**Andy, Terry and Jill love watching the TV show:**

○ a) *Elephant on a Bicycle*
○ b) *Tiger on a Tricycle*
○ c) *Hippo on a Hovercraft*
○ d) *Mr Big Nose on a Boogie Board*

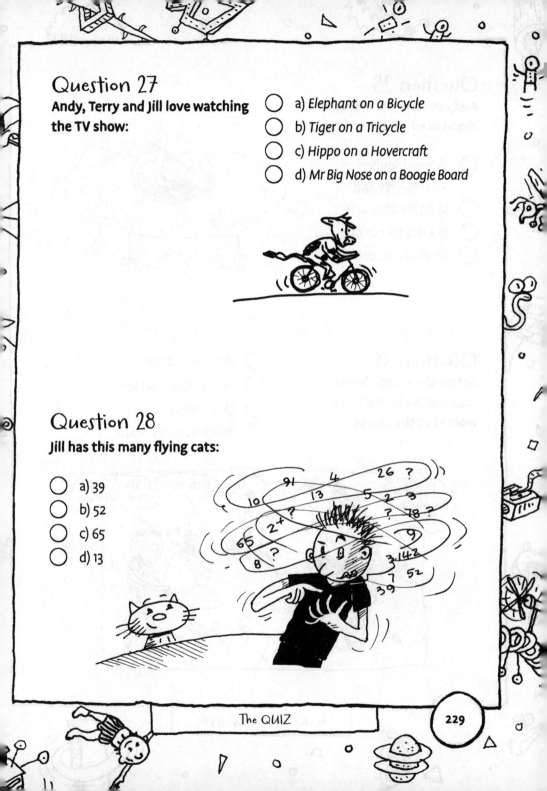

## Question 28

**Jill has this many flying cats:**

○ a) 39
○ b) 52
○ c) 65
○ d) 13

## Question 29
**Andy and Terry travelled to the moon in which type of rocket?**

- ○ a) one disguised as a flying fried egg
- ○ b) an invisible one
- ○ c) a dot-to-dot one
- ○ d) an electric one

## Question 30
**Before they made books together Andy and Terry worked at the zoo in:**

- ○ a) the gift shop
- ○ b) the education unit
- ○ c) the office
- ○ d) the monkey house

I hate monkey poo.

Ha. Ha!

Shut up and sweep.

## Answers
(Score one point for each correct answer)

**1. If Mr Big Nose gets angry:**
c) his nose gets bigger and bigger

**2. Andyland is:**
b) the Andy-est place on Earth

**3. Professor Stupido is:**
b) an UN-inventor

**4. Barky the Barking Dog likes to:**
a) bark

**5. Terry has a pair of emergency inflatable:**
b) underpants

**6. What does the marshmallow machine shoot into your mouth?**
d) marshmallows

**7. If you lost a sausage, you would look for it in:**
c) the lost sausage office

**8. You get to Banarnia by:**
a) going through the wardrobe on top of the garbage dump

**9. When Captain Woodenhead loses his head, he carves a new one out of:**
c) wood

**10. Silky is:**
d) all of the above (a catnary, a flying cat and Jill's favourite pet)

**11. Vegetable Patty's parents were killed by giant:**
b) vegetables

**12. The ATM on level 21 is an:**
d) Automatic Tattoo Machine

**13. Prince Potato rules over a kingdom of:**
c) vegetables

**14. How many flavours of ice-cream does Edward Scooperhands have in the ice-cream parlour?**
a) 78

**15. Jill's three horses are called:**
b) Larry, Curly and Moe

WHO? WHAT? WHERE?

**16. Which of these is NOT a prize on the spin-and-win prize wheel?**
a) a year's supply of cat food

**17. The money-making machine also makes:**
c) honey

**18. If you visited the planet Eyeballia, you would see a lot of:**
b) giant flying eyeballs

**19. The official name of Terry's long-distance talking device is:**
a) super-flexible, endlessly extendable, titanium-coated talking tube

**20. The softest and safest level in the treehouse is:**
d) the room full of pillows

**21. Andy and Terry hate:**
d) all of the above (monkeys, pirates and vegetables)

**22. Andy and Terry love:**
d) none of the above (monkeys, pirates and vegetables)

**23. Anti-Andy, Terrible-Terry and Junkyard-Jill are:**
a) Andy, Terry and Jill's doppelgangers

**24. The treehouse disabled-access ramp is:**
d) the most exciting one in the world

**25. Everything on the Filing Island has been filed:**
b) alphabetically

**26. Andy's high-security potato chip safe is protected by:**
e) all of the above (1000 loaded mousetraps, 100 laser beams, a 10-tonne weight and a very angry duck)

**27. Andy, Terry and Jill love watching the TV show:**

a) *Elephant on a Bicycle*

**28. Jill has this many flying cats:**

d) 13

**29. Andy and Terry travelled to the moon in which type of rocket?**

c) a dot-to-dot one

**30. Before they made books together Andy and Terry worked at the zoo in:**

d) the monkey house

WHO? WHAT? WHERE?

# Results

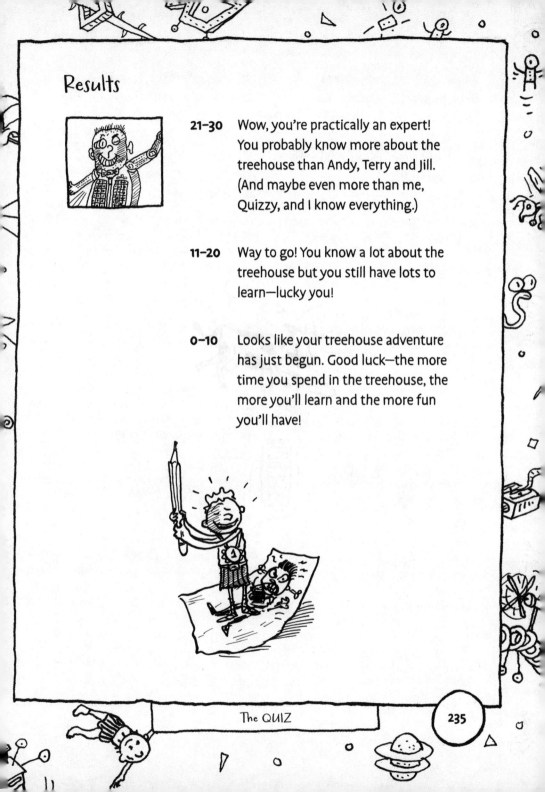

**21–30**  Wow, you're practically an expert! You probably know more about the treehouse than Andy, Terry and Jill. (And maybe even more than me, Quizzy, and I know everything.)

**11–20**  Way to go! You know a lot about the treehouse but you still have lots to learn—lucky you!

**0–10**  Looks like your treehouse adventure has just begun. Good luck—the more time you spend in the treehouse, the more you'll learn and the more fun you'll have!